Misplaced and Forgotten

W.J. Thompson

Copyright © 2023 W.J.Thompson

All Rights Reserved

ISBN-13: 979-8-3492-1813-2

Misplaced and Forgotten

1

I don't want to sound ungrateful and start a story by complaining, but there's no other way around it.

The afterlife can feel hollow at times.

I know, I know, how can anyone find a way to complain about heaven? Let me explain. I'm not saying it isn't great. It feels damn near perfect, outside of a few minor annoyances. There's no lack of people to see or places to go. You can do pretty much whatever you want (within reason). However, there are times when you can feel that something is not quite right. The excited confusion after my death led to a long stretch of blissful euphoria, so it wasn't until I began looking back on my own time among the living that I was able to get an idea of what was missing here. Still, it took me a while to put the feeling into words. I realized it wasn't something tangible; it was the lack of consequences for your actions, that sense of weight that comes with the choices you make every day while alive. It just feels different when there's the possibility of making a wrong choice.

I was at a loss for how to fix the issue. Complaining about heaven being too perfect? I assumed there had to be something wrong with me.

Fortunately, I was able to speak with someone who knew me better than anyone else in the universe—my conscience. Some of the people I knew while alive believed that my mind was slipping, but that is not a euphemism for talking to myself. And no, I did not have a talkative pet cricket, either.

Let me explain.

Every person born is assigned a previously lived soul as their personal inner guide. Mine was Peter. Although I didn't know it at the time, he was there with me through every one of my many mistakes and influenced all three of my smart decisions. After his death, I often came to him for advice. When I relayed my feelings on consequences to him, his advice was as simple and eloquent as I had come to expect from him.

"Then get off ye arse and do something that matters."

His words, although sometimes abrasive, proved to be helpful. As we spoke, he told me about how he was once in a similar mindset, loving the afterlife but feeling like something was lacking, when he decided to take on the role of a conscience. He told me it might be good to head back and take on one of the grandest responsibilities. Plus, it might add a little excitement and adventure to my existence. So, after spending a few centuries in the afterlife, I made the bold decision to find the purpose and meaning that had been missing.

I signed up with the Earth Affairs agent and soon found myself escorted to the long line of souls waiting to return to Earth. Many of us were heading there for the first time since our deaths, so we had some very informative classes to complete. There was an expansive amount to learn, and it didn't take long for me to feel completely overwhelmed.

For starters, our role was much more broad than just being the little voice of reason in the back of someone's mind. Our primary job would be that of a transcriber, jotting down every minute detail of our person's life and placing the books into a personal library to reference when particular memories were needed. I knew from frequent trips to my life library that this part of the work was going to be a challenge. However, we were not limited by the constructs of Earthly physics. Physical space would be a little more forgiving, as was the language we would be writing with. It is nearly impossible to describe it to someone who has not seen it before. The best attempt I can make is that the words are not just stagnant collections of letters but alive with shape and form and action. To give an example, when you see the word "door" written, you may think of a solid piece of wood or metal that denotes the entrance or exit of a given place. It opens and closes and usually has a handle. You can probably picture one without much more information. However, when written with the language of the afterlife that same word would denote the exact color, texture, sound, smell, feel, age, history, and every other seemingly unnoticed detail of a particular door. You would see every little scratch, hear even the smallest creak, and feel the tiniest paint chips, all just from that single word. It allows us to chronicle all the billions of details that our person experiences daily but may not even realize exist.

Still with me?

I was told that my person would be matched with my personality as best as could be predicted. Given that I was an Englishman who died in the New World in 1789 after a long, albeit difficult life, I would be matched to a male, born in the United States of America around the late 20th century, who may also have a difficult life, for one reason or another. The thinking behind this policy was that our own life experiences might help guide us to be more helpful voices of reason. It made sense, and, for the most part, it worked for thousands and thousands of years before I ever arrived. Peter, my own conscience, had been a resident of the British Isles who died at the hand of a lord's tax collector. He may have influenced my feelings about the government. Hard to say for sure.

No need to delve into my own boring past right now, though. This is not my story.

After being told the somewhat vague details about my person, we were all given updates on what life was currently like on Earth. There were no big surprises. Since time still moves in the same linear fashion in the afterlife, many of us enjoy peeking in on what's happening down there. And lately, it seemed dull moments were few and far between. One decade, someone invents a horseless carriage that travels with some unseen power. It was remarkable. Then, not all that long after, a couple of brothers build a pair of wings, carrying them off the ground for a few hundred feet. It was an even more amazing accomplishment! Humans lifted off into the sky like a great gliding albatross! But then, just a couple of decades and many advancements later, it is decided that both of these modern marvels should also have weapons attached, and many more souls would end up here well before their time because of it. That has seemed to be a sad pattern for humans. Come up with an amazing invention capable of moving humanity closer towards each other and then figuring out how it could best be used to end other people's lives quicker.

But I digress.

After hearing all about highways and disco and the space shuttle and Star Wars, we moved on to the rules we had to follow. They seemed simple enough. Common sense, really. I couldn't announce my presence. I had to keep track of everything that happened in my person's waking life. I was allowed to guide them in their decision-making but act only as a voice of reason. My influence had to be kept minimal. There could be no getting in the way of free will. None of the rules seemed too difficult to follow, so I may have stopped paying attention.

We were given warnings about what happens when those rules were broken though. If a conscience became a bit too vocal as an inner voice, you could drive your person to a state of insanity. If you decided that you didn't feel like chronicling your person's days anymore, they would have no memory of them. If you give bad advice, like telling your person they should act out in violence, then they may just listen to you and hurt others. There were so many ways we could ruin our person's life and they all centered around putting our needs before theirs. It was something I took very seriously. Punishments for those that hurt their person were terrible. Smaller misdeeds may only lead to having to live a life as a dung beetle or worm. However, some faced the worst possible consequence. Permanent banishment of your soul.

Scary stuff.

By the time I was told that my person was going to be born soon, I was feeling pretty nervous. I wanted to make sure I was the best possible guide for the new soul. But what if I was assigned someone who never listened to my advice? What if I didn't like them? I knew that the powers-that-be were careful about matching us together, but they weren't infallible. I mean, this is heaven, so I guess they were, but I still had the same cynical skepticism of those in charge that I always had.

Fortunately, the soul I was matched with was a good one, but that didn't make the job any easier.

David Alexander Zinski was my first assignment as a conscience. Once I got there, I realized the first few years were not the cakewalk I expected. This was before David had developed the ability to grasp any of the advice I'd try to give him. I spent so much time nervously watching and yelling things like "FIRE HOT" or "DON'T PUT THE KEYS IN THE ELECTRICAL SOCKET." It was pointless, though. During these years, David had to learn things the hard way, and all I could do was watch and write down what I saw. Thankfully, the burnt hands healed, and any electrocutions were minor. Things got a little better once he was able to start making logical decisions, but my advice was not often heeded. He was just as headstrong as I had been. Poor decisions would compound on each other, and, at times, he would feel buried. His own feelings of disappointment would drown out my voice. It was a vicious cycle. Thankfully, he had great friends who always helped him get through the toughest times.

Until he decided he wasn't worthy of their love anymore.

And all of that brings me to the book you are currently reading.

I decided that if I was going to spend so much time filling countless pages with every little detail of David's life, then I was going to need a hobby, and it might as well be writing about my experiences. I focused on writing something that I might want to read and share after this assignment. The late 20th to early 21st century was a pretty exciting time, and there were plenty of things I wanted to record and reflect on. This is the very abridged version (no one wants to read a thirty-eight thousand-page opus filled with the bored ramblings of a long-dead man). It covers an event that transpired during David's life that was as rare and unexpected as it was life-altering.

What follows is the story of the time that David learned all about me and his library.

2

Waves crashed not far from the idyllic, white-sanded coastline. David stood there watching, feeling the tide rise to his knees and then down to his ankles. The perfectly blue, choppy water created a jagged, warped mirror of the few clouds passing overhead. The bright midday sun was unforgiving, but he didn't mind it much. Feeling the heat on his bare arms and back was always the perfect precursor to jumping in the tepid water. A smile stretched across his face as he closed his eyes and absorbed all of the sounds and smells of his favorite place. He heard his friends calling out to him from up on the dune, telling him to join them. He went to turn and go to them but found he couldn't move. His smile disappeared. The gritty, wet sand felt like it was slowly pulling him down each time the rising water rushed back to the ocean. The current felt like it was getting stronger, the ocean grabbing hold of his legs. A wave of mild panic crept into the place where his happiness had just been residing.

Suddenly he blinked, and it was dark. A full moon replaced the blinding sun. The sounds of his friends were gone, replaced now with the deafening crash of thundering waves all around him. The water was higher, reaching up to his chest. He thought he could hear a woman's voice just barely audible over the roar. He couldn't make out what she was saying, but it felt familiar like he had been here before. As his eyes adjusted to the darkness, he noticed something in the water. A dark silhouette stood far from the shore, just visible beyond the moonlit cresting waves. He wanted to go to her but he was stuck motionless, looking out into the blackness of the angry sea, body frozen...

EHHHH—EHHHH—EHHHHH—EHH...

David lay there for a moment, eyes still closed, cursing the alarm clock. He despised the sudden interruption to his dreams. They were his nightly escape from a boring, lonely life, and the feeling of being violently yanked away from them felt unnatural and not something any sane person could ever get used to. Even after years of enduring this, he never looked at it with anything less than disdain. There was no other way, though. It was an unfortunate side effect of having to go to work. To pay bills. To survive. He hated all of it. To him, it took the best things about waking up, slowly getting acclimated to the start of a new day, peacefully transitioning from the dream world to the real one, and hitting them all repeatedly with a baseball bat until they were just swollen, misshapen lumps of broken happiness.

He couldn't shake the sense that there was something about the dream he was just having that felt important. He tried gently backtracking in his mind, searching for a breadcrumb to follow, to find his way to the trail he was on just before that damn alarm clock roared to life. The feeling felt familiar like he'd had the same waking-up-lost-and-angry feeling before, but the trail was cold. He let it go, frustrated about everything, and he wasn't even fully awake yet.

Bodes well for the rest of the day.

He realized a long time ago that his dreams were becoming increasingly the high point of his day, and the struggle to leave them each morning was a growing challenge. No matter what they were about, they at least gave his life some break from the monotony that consumed his every waking moment. Even the dreams he struggled to remember, like the one from last night, found a way to leave clues for his mind to try and follow, making him long to return to sleep and find his way back to the place he had left. There would probably be some flashes of memories or deja vu or thoughts of his old life that would pop up while doing some trivial task at work, and before he knew it, he would be lost in another daydream.

But it was these times in the morning, the moments when the line between dreams and real life was blurred and hard to define, that became the biggest struggle. Everything around him seemed to be conspiring against his fully joining the world of the awake.

His pillow was silky soft and always cool, inviting him to close his eyes and stay just a little longer. As he rolled over, away from the early morning light peaking through his curtains, he wrapped himself a little tighter, finding solace in the warm embrace of his thick winter blanket. Spring had arrived slowly this year, and even though the mornings of frost-covered grass were finally coming to an end, there was still plenty of chill in the air.

The room was quiet. Only some soft morning sounds slipped into his window. His ears caught the light-muffled melody of birds singing outside. His apartment was on the third floor and there were a few just-budding oak trees not far from his bedroom window. He loved sleeping with it open just a crack to let some of the cold in at night. Once winter ended, it had an added benefit. The sounds of life starting up, the beautiful cacophony of singing birds, chirping bugs, and distant traffic, would be clearer and pleasant to his slowly waking ears. It was a nice contrast to the loud ringing of an over-eager alarm.

He laid there with a growing desire to drift back to that hauntingly quiet sleep he had been enjoying. *Maybe just for a few more minutes...*

EHHHH—EHHHH—EHHH...

Fine, I'm up, He thought to himself. Damn snooze button. The time between alarms never seemed consistent. Some mornings, it felt like it stretched out for hours, and he would get great sleep between those 8 minutes. Not today, though. Even with his mind swimming in a sea of random thoughts, it seemed to him that the alarms happened almost concurrently. He didn't see any point in delaying the inevitable. It was time to break through the peacefulness and safety of his homemade cocoon.

David reluctantly opened his eyes, scowled at the clock, instinctually grabbed his phone, and began scrolling through the news, drawn into random stories about other people's more exciting lives. It was mindless and meaningless, and he wasn't even sure why he did it, and yet, no matter what he would tell himself the night before about waking up with a purpose, about doing something better, it was still the first thing he did after reluctantly deciding not to go back to sleep. Much like his dreams, he wouldn't remember most of the stories once he was out of bed. Just bits and pieces of pollution for his mind.

After way too much half-asleep scrolling, he put his phone down and kicked off his covers.

He lay there, cold and frustrated, and groggily looked around the room, eyes trudging through the mix of earth tones. Browns, blues, greens. The dresser and nightstands were made to look like they were crafted from logs, and there was a large rug around the bed that resembled grass. Some paintings of forests and beaches and mountains decorated the walls. He had long loved the outdoors and felt that with his limited time to explore and limited friends to encourage him to get outside, that passion for nature was now bleeding through his stylistic tendencies instead. He didn't have any pets to take care of, but plenty of plants were scattered throughout the apartment. If he wasn't going out to experience it, at least he could look around and remind himself of the things he loved. It felt safer that way.

He finally pulled together enough energy to lift himself out of bed and trudged down the hallway and into the bathroom. A glance into the mirror made him pause. No matter how often he saw him, the man in the reflection still didn't feel familiar. David always pictured himself as the young, vibrant man from his memories. The face staring back at him was rounder, with gray hair creeping just above his ears. Small wrinkles around the eyes. A growing belly. He shook his head and made the same bound-to-be-broken promise he had repeated countless times before: *I'm going to start taking better care of myself.*

Lies.

He turned on the shower and waited for it to get to a temp just below scalding. The gray-white steam rising above the shower curtain looked like storm clouds forming. The slightly-too-hot water always did the trick, though. This was typically when his brain would finally begin turning on for the day. The morning fog that clouded his head was starting to get burned off. Not completely, mind you, but at least enough to think about the day ahead. He mapped out how it would go. There would be the usual daydream-fueled drive to work. That would be followed by an overwhelmingly boring 8 hours of sitting at his desk. Then a peaceful drive home before wrapping up his day by watching TV or reading a book or playing on his phone or some other activity where he could shut off his mind and simply zone out. Then he would be right back in his warm and cozy bed. He wasn't even out of the shower yet, and the thought of going back to sleep was the first thing that made him crack a smile. He finished washing up, got dressed, grabbed a pop tart, made some coffee. The same order of activities he followed every morning. He was able to get through all of this on autopilot.

He got in his slightly worn down, ten-year-old black-and-rust colored Honda Accord and started it up. The car wasn't in the best shape, but who is once they get a bunch of miles on them? It was good enough for him as long as he could play his music. He started to eat a pop tart while scrolling through the playlists on his phone. He loved music but never really updated his library. His tastes were frozen in time. The songs reminded him of a more carefree version of himself when he had close friends and a life that was rarely the same from one day to the next. He started up his car as Bitter Sweet Symphony by The Verve began playing. The song brought on memories of friends drunkenly belting out the lyrics while sitting around a bonfire. The sounds of their off-key notes rattled around his head. It felt like it happened in a completely different lifetime.

A better one.

Zoning out to the music was like taking shots of nostalgia-laced trips, but they were just appetizers. Daydreaming was the main course. This was mostly because, just like his time asleep each night, he let his mind wander wherever it cared to go. The only downside (you know, other than the whole not-paying-attention-while-driving thing) was that it always felt like it was over too soon. He would be so lost in the memories of better days that he would suddenly find himself pulling into his parking space at work.

This morning was no different, and so the reminiscing of his days of drunken debauchery would have to be put on pause for now.

Arriving at the office was always the second lowest point of his day, just barely behind the nagging alarm, and this morning felt doubly bad. It was only Wednesday. He knew he was staring down at least eight hours of mind-numbingly boring work. His cubicle was at the end of a long row of drab blandness. Some coworkers had tried bringing color into their open-air jail cells, but it always felt like they were swallowed up by the all-consuming light gray/off-white color palette. He imagined that the colors were chosen to ensure any small amount of joy in the workplace was snuffed out. It was very effective.

The hours spent sitting in his cubicle were boring, tedious, and above all, lonely. Most days, he would get away with not talking to any of his cellmates. That's what he considered all of his coworkers. Prisoners. They were all trapped in a system that they could never escape. Most just never let those thoughts in, but David couldn't help it. He was in a constant battle against the urge to get up and leave and do something else more rewarding with his day. However, leaving your job early just because you felt like it was usually frowned upon.

He considered quitting at least once every few weeks. Never more serious than just a passing thought, though. As much as it felt like the job was slowly sucking away all his remaining time on the planet, the fear of the unknown was scarier. He had spent some time after college bouncing from one job to the next and never really felt like he had financially caught up to his peers. When it came to money, he was walking a tightrope with no net. He was never really able to put aside any savings, so taking time off to find something more personally fulfilling was out of the question. This job paid him enough to have his lonely apartment and live his quiet, lonely life. So he would push those thoughts out of his head and just keep trudging along.

This wasn't anywhere near how he pictured his life when he was young and idealistic. He had lots of friends. Big dreams. He was going to be somebody important who did important things and made everyone's life better. He may not have known exactly what that something would be, but he knew he was going to be good at it and have fun doing it. He was a typical idealistic dreamer. Back then, he didn't see a point in wasting time with anything that didn't make you happy. Somewhere along the way…or, maybe, at many points along the way…the wrong choice was made, and he slowly found himself more and more alone and just doing enough to get by. Oh well.

Such is life.

As much as he tried to avoid thinking about it, the fact remained that it had been a long time since he felt anything resembling real happiness. But that's not to say he was always sad, either. Just sort of in the middle. He realized long ago that life rarely goes how you plan, and you can either fight it or accept it. He fought it at first but, after a while, gave up and just chose to accept his lonely fate. He couldn't remember when that exact moment occurred. Probably around the time he moved away from his friends. The thing that helped him come to terms with all of this was when he realized that no matter what problems he had to face in his real life, he had an escape in his dreams, and they were where he could live whatever life he wanted.

Having such an uneventful waking life combined with a very active imagination often made his work day extra painful. He sometimes thought that if his younger self could have written about his most pitiful, depressing possible future, David was sure he would be pretty close to living it now. Boring job. Complete lack of a social life. Distant friends and family that he hadn't spoken to in who-knows-how-long. And don't even get started on the completely missing love life. He gave up trying to improve those things a long time ago.

Even though he had been working in the same place for almost a decade, he didn't know anyone too well. There were mandatory office meetings and random social events where he would interact, as politely as he could, with his coworkers. Some seemed really nice. But he tried to avoid engaging in small talk or starting up conversations, and the old invites for office parties were almost always left un-replied. The only person who ever seemed to notice this was his boss. Almost like clockwork, he would come around and make sure that David had seen the invite and try to talk him into coming. He would periodically ask him to come out for a beer or to watch a game at a pub up the street. David always had an excuse. He was perfectly content to stay in his cubicle, finish his work, and then return home.

Not really, though.

Work started, and David switched his autopilot back on. There were no meetings scheduled. The morning emails only consisted of one about some new hires and another about an upcoming birthday get-together for a coworker. David disregarded the first one but opened the second. The email said that the office was getting together to celebrate "Kathy's Third Annual 39th Birthday Party," and he knew he would have to come up with a good excuse to miss it. He decided that was a later problem and got to work.

Most of the day went by in a blur. He was so busy bouncing between daydreaming and staring blankly at his computer that he didn't even realize he had worked through his lunch. He was surviving on pop tarts, caffeine, and the motivation to leave on time. Around 2 pm, he decided to grab another coffee from the break room and maybe snag something from the vending machine. He passed by a few coworkers talking around the copier. Jared, Allison, and Ricky. This was the group that spearheaded all the get-togethers. The cool kids of the office. He overheard them talking about some upcoming bar excursion they were planning. Jared gave him a small smile and nod as he passed. He was thankful he didn't get roped into an awkward conversation.

After the short break, he was back at his desk. Mercifully, the next few hours passed without him even noticing, and before he knew it, he was logging off and packing up for the day.

He went down the long row of prison-cell gray cubicles without so much as a "see ya tomorrow" or "have a good one". His feelings of loneliness had been dulled over the years. Where these slights used to feel like stabs to his gut, now the daily reminders were simply little pokes in his chest. He was able to brush off those feelings quickly since he would soon be in his car and could go back to zoning out to some good music.

The drive home consisted of bumper-to-bumper traffic for an hour. Years ago, this was a source of supreme frustration, but now he found he actually enjoyed it. *Better than being at my desk*, David thought. In reality, it wasn't much of a step up though, still trapped sitting in a box focused on the task in front of him, but at least he could control his music and lose himself in a daydream.

So pretty much exactly like sitting at his desk.

As he slowly crept up the curve of the on-ramp, his mind drifted back to more memories of good times with his friends, back when his life had more to it than just sleep and work, with brief slivers of dreaming in between. There were times he would get so frustrated for not being happy. That feeling was creeping into his mind right now, but he fought back against it. His past was over and done with, and he had to focus on being fortunate enough to have lived those days. At least that's what the little voice in the back of his mind would say. David wasn't sure if having those great memories made things worse now.

As he pulled into the parking lot of his apartment, he was still dwelling on those good old days. Literally thinking to himself, *ahh, those were the good old days*. Then rolled his eyes when he realized he was referring to anything from his past as "the good old days."

His apartment was not fancy by any stretch of the imagination. It would best be politely described as "cozy". He prized comfort and durability over style and substance and so his furniture was a mismatch of dark-stained wood tables and shelves and light brown fabric couches and chairs. A large window in the middle of the room gave him an unobstructed view of the few oak trees that sprang up at the edge of the parking lot. Once spring fully arrived, probably just a few weeks from now, the green leaves would block out any view of the asphalt. He kept a large variety of plants scattered around, but the majority of them were in front of that window. It gave life to what otherwise felt like a lifeless room. The shelves along the walls in his living room were littered with small knick-knacks, pictures of his friends and family, and some of his favorite books. All relics of his past, a small shrine to the life he lived before. The one splash of color in the room was a large sky blue and forest green rug in the middle of the room. *It really ties the room together*, he thought, quoting a movie he hadn't watched since college.

The few hours he had each evening between the time he ate dinner and the time he laid down in bed were spent lost in some form of easily consumable entertainment. Maybe some movie or TV show that caught his eye, but more often, he would find himself lost in a familiar book. He loved the temporary escape from reality; a good book could take him to completely different worlds.

Tonight, he stretched out on his couch and grabbed a personal favorite from his bookshelf. *Galapagos* by Kurt Vonnegut. The binding was worn and frayed from the amount of times David had re-read it. He knew the story well and always enjoyed the way it was told by a ghost disconnectedly watching the major events unfold. He had felt like his life was playing out in a similar way. Viewing his friends and family's lives from a distance on social media, never really interacting but still hoping everything worked out for the best. He loved them all, even if he felt they had long forgotten him.

Time and distance can do that.

He got so into reading the first few chapters that he was shocked to look up at his clock and notice it was almost midnight. It was time to crawl into his lonely bed and get lost in some hopefully exciting dreams before waking up and repeating the cycle again.

His head hit the pillow with thoughts firmly on some good memories of his distant friends. He hoped that would get his dreams going in a positive direction. Eyes closed, he thought back to a time when he and his three closest friends spent a day on the beach together. There were so many of them to choose from, but one always stood out from the others. He was young, just barely a teenager. It was the first time they had all gone with no adult supervision. All these years later, the details were covered in a thick haze, but a few strong feelings kept the memory alive. The sun beating mercilessly down on him...the feeling of total freedom...and noticing real beauty for the first time as the sunset.

David fell asleep, his mind drifting toward places and people no longer in his life but never fully leaving it.

3

I gently placed my worn-down pencil on the desk. Another unremarkable day finished. I picked up the completed book and made my way through the labyrinth of bookshelves. Over the years, the shelves grew into bookcases, the bookcases into full walls, and then the room slowly expanded to allow more and more rows. There are times I catch myself looking proudly at all the books I've written. Well, transcribed, really. David was the one who controlled the narrative. But it still feels like an accomplishment, tracking every little detail of his life.

There was nothing special about today's addition to the library, but at least no new problems or poorly thought-out decisions were made. Being able to check both of those imaginary boxes, no matter how many times I did it, always felt like an accomplishment. Admittedly, the bar I set was low, but I considered that to be more a reflection of David's past trauma than any indictment of his character.

He always did the best he could. Or the best he knew how to do.

Still though, and I hate even to admit it, I can't help but be bored out of my mind at the life he's chosen. I feel terrible complaining about his choices, especially since I'm supposed to be the one guiding him. Bang up job, Matthew, right?

Don't answer that.

Now there is nothing wrong with wanting a life of peace, but I just don't understand why he won't even try something, anything, to change up his days. He used to keep me on my toes, trying to follow his social life. But now, there are days when he doesn't even speak, not a single word, to anyone but himself. Quiet solitude is great in small doses. Too much of it, though, and you begin to lose the very things that make you alive. That's been the case with David for far too long. Life is about so much more than just eating and breathing and being awake. It's friends and family and love and pain and adventure and experiences...

My apologies. I think I might be experiencing some underlying afterlife frustration. They have a saying up in heaven, a variation of one I knew well during the later years of my Earth-bound life.

Life is wasted on the living.

I would be lying if I tried to say my own life had been crazy and exciting, and there were plenty of regrets about that. Peter had told me how, no matter what he thought, his job was to chronicle my life and safely steer me toward one that afforded me as much time as possible. Everything else was up to me. I try to remember that when I feel like banging my head against my desk. If I hadn't taken up writing as a hobby, I'm not sure I would've made it past David's thirtieth birthday.

I wrote a "David's Average Day" edition that could replace pretty much any of the last few hundred days, and no one would even notice. It was a collection of his most recent mind-numbingly dull daily routines. I put it together one night to try to slip into his dreams, hoping that he might wake up and realize how amazingly uneventful his life had become.

No such luck.

After waking up, David simply went about his day like he always did, daydreaming about his old friends while functioning with little mental effort. I used to worry that he would stumble on one particularly traumatic period from his past with how much he would think about those days gone by. It took much effort on my part to shield him from having to relive that pain. Without being able to watch his dreams, I can never know for sure if any of those memories rise to the surface, but if they do, he hasn't given them much thought in his waking life.

Hell, maybe he needs to relive something like that just to know he can still feel anything at all.

But being the old softy that I am, pushing him toward happier memories was the route I typically went. I could tell his friends were filling his thoughts more than usual lately. I made sure to lay out a couple of his favorite dream magazines, ones that included his hometown beach and some pleasant memories. I liked being able to guide his small, nightly escapes. I didn't have absolute control, but I did have the ability to give him a little push in the right direction.

I waited at the end of the last bookshelf and saw David arrive on the couch, grab the magazine on the top of the stack, and disappear into a hopefully happy dream.

I waited for a moment before slipping today's edition into its place on the last bookshelf. One day, hopefully, decades from now, David will walk this library, picking out his favorite days and revisiting his happiest memories. I look forward to seeing him smile again.

4

The sky was painted with a blend of vibrant purples, orangish yellows, and deep, dark reds. The sun was setting but not in the active sense of the word. It was as if it were on pause at the precise moment that its rays gave the horizon its breathtaking hues. David took a sip of his beer while his friends, Jimmy and Drew, were trying to get a fire started. A few unrecognizable faces were sitting in beach chairs, talking. Someone had a guitar and the sound was filling the space between his friend's words. He felt a gentle hand on his shoulder followed by a soft whisper in his ear.

"Hey, handsome," came a familiar voice.

But he couldn't place where he had heard it before. He turned and saw the most beautiful woman he had ever laid eyes on. She had blonde hair and bright blue eyes that locked with his as she smiled at him and slipped her hand into his. He smiled, too, looking at what felt like the perfect evening. He closed his eyes and ...

EHHHH—EHHHH—EHHH...

The next morning was the same as the hundreds of others that came before it. Alarm. Snooze. Shower. Dressed. Pop tart. Coffee. The only part that provided a bit of variety was the dreams. Always the dreams. He couldn't remember everything about the one he was having last night but some little bits of memory hung around his mind the way a sweet scent will still linger after baking cookies. He knew his friends were there and that it was at the beach. Beyond that, nothing. He woke up with a sense of happy nostalgia combined with some distant feeling of sadness. It wasn't a surprise, given how often his thoughts found their way to the good times he used to have, coupled with the loneliness he'd fought off since leaving his friends.

My dreams are ghosts, he thought, *whispering reminders of a life that died a long time ago.*

He knew he had to be careful with the rabbit hole these thoughts could drop him into. Thinking about his old life too much had sent him spiraling into a series of deep depressions on a few occasions. The first was not long after moving up here. He didn't even realize what was happening until it was too late. Caught up thinking about all the formerly familiar places and the formerly familiar people that he missed, and then, seemingly out of nowhere, came an emotional crash. He spent the next few months trying to shake the sadness and despair. The same mistake was made on a couple of other occasions until he finally developed a sense of what was happening and when he should dial back the reminiscing.

Not such an easy task when, in his current life, every day felt like an overplayed record, with the little things that used to bring some small amount of happiness slowly worn down. The loud notes just didn't strike a chord anymore. Some days felt like nothing but static. Drinking heavily helped, but he couldn't handle the days-long, excruciating hangovers anymore. Letting his daydreams take over became his preferred method of sober survival.

With a pop tart in one hand and a coffee in the other, he got in the car and had his typical mind-anywhere-but-here drive to work. Today's thought topics veered from his old high school friends to moving in with them and living an awesome bachelor life, to his last girlfriend. It was like each set of memories was connected by strings, but when he got to the last one, it was nothing but a frayed, cut end. He vaguely remembered dating someone a few years back when he was finishing up college but couldn't recall anything about her. It felt strange.

Oh well.

He pulled into work with his mind still trailing far behind, somewhere between the bed he was longing to be back in and the life he wished he was still living. It seemed to snap back into place once he shut his car door and began walking to the office building. There were some out-of-place flowers that he first noticed the week before. Not many but those few small hints of color growing up out of the edge of the dead, gray pavement had caught his eye, and he took their tenacity as a sign of hope. Little pieces of life peeking through an otherwise lifeless slab of asphalt. David found beauty in these types of things. He slowed his walk so that he could hold on to the mental image of those sun-soaked yellow and white flowers. The small smile he gained from the persistent little guys hung with him on his walk to his cubicle, even after he was slapped in the face with the complete visual opposite of lively colors.

As he walked down the trail of sterile-ness, he saw his boss waiting at his desk. He didn't take this as a bad sign or anything like that. Tom was a nice enough guy. He would come by to talk to David every few weeks, checking in and making small talk. David gave a weak nod of acknowledgment as he approached.

Tom may have looked the part, but his personality was not one that ever struck him as being the stereotypical boss. He was middle-aged with short hair going around his head, circling the shiny bald spot on top. He had a short, graying beard that was always walking a thin line between well-groomed and rambling. He seemed to be constantly masking his stress with a forced smile. He was slightly shorter than David and a bit more round and had always seemed like he was just a bit too pleasant to be working in management. David had plenty of bosses in the past that led with intimidation or condescension. Tom was a welcome change, even if he tried a little too hard sometimes.

"Morning, David!" He said with a peppiness that felt unnatural this early.

"Morning, Tom. What can I do for you?" David asked while trying, unsuccessfully, to return a forced smile. Damn. Yesterday's email invite. He forgot to respond.

"I wasn't sure if you saw the emails...", He knew I saw them, "...and wanted to let you know that the team is going out for drinks after work to celebrate Kathy's birthday. I figured you might have just gotten too busy and forgotten to reply." As much as David appreciated that his boss went out of his way to deliver the intentionally avoided RSVPs, it would turn into a mental scramble to find a quick excuse. He completely spaced on figuring out a good reason not to go to this one, so just said the first thing that came to mind.

"I'm sorry, Tom. I'm behind on a few things and was planning on staying late today. I'll make sure to stop by her desk later to wish her a happy birthday." That was weak, and David knew it, but he couldn't think of anything else. He figured, what boss wouldn't want one of their employees to work some extra time?

"Are you sure? You know, you are one of the most productive members of the team, so falling a little behind isn't going to kill you," Tom responded in the most un-boss-like way possible.

"No, no, it's alright. I prefer being a little ahead of my work. Less stress, you know. Maybe next time." David knew he would have to come up with a better excuse before the next office get-together. He made a mental note to check the work calendar and see how long until the next birthday, work anniversary, or other random holiday the team would want to celebrate.

"Yeah, yeah, I know. Well, the invitation is there if you change your mind. We'll be at the Irish pub by the library. You should try to come by after you finish up here." David knew Tom's intentions were well-meaning, but he didn't want an awkward night out with co-workers.

"I'll consider it," David lied. Tom gave a knowing nod and patted the edge of the cubicle as he turned and walked away. David knew that at some point he would have to suck it up and go out and he knew that he just might have a little fun too. But then his coworkers would start expecting him to socialize, and they'd come by his cubicle to make small talk and start asking about his life, and then they'd probably start trying to set him up with some single friend...it would all get terribly messy, and he did not want to go anywhere near that road.

After briefly considering and just as quickly squashing the thought of being social, David sat at his desk and got started on his work. It was hard to focus though. He thought some of his coworkers seemed pretty cool, but he had done a damn good job of not developing any new relationships since moving up here, and he wanted to keep it that way. He worked right through his lunch break (again) and, after a quick snack, threw his headphones on and focused all his energy on work. The time passed abnormally fast. When he saw it was after 6, and everyone else had already left, he decided to grab a quick bite to eat. *A few more hours and I'll be good to go*, he thought.

For all the downsides of staying in the office as the day turned to night, staying late at work did have a few benefits. The office was empty, which allowed him to take his headphones off and turn the music up. He could even sing along, and no one would complain about the weird screeching coming from his cubicle. On very rare occasions, usually after consuming way too much coffee, he would walk the rows of cubicles, making sure that no one was there.

And then crank the music as loud as his little speaker would go and dance. At least 'dance' was the word that came to mind. A more accurate description would be highly caffeinated convulsions.

By being the only living soul in the office, he could pretend he wasn't so antisocial that he still lived a life outside of his head. Forgetting, even for a brief moment, that so many years had passed since he had fun. It was ironic that the moments he spent in the office alone were the closest he felt to his old, gregarious self.

He spent the next couple of hours zoned out in a mix of musical nostalgia and work-related spreadsheets. Once the numbers seemed to start bouncing to the beat of the songs, he knew it was time to finally call it a day. He packed up his briefcase and headed for the exit.

He made his way down to the parking lot and stopped as he walked near the few lonely flowers that he passed this morning. They were still beautiful, even without the sunlight glistening off their colorful petals. He bent down and almost plucked one from its stem before thinking better of it and grabbing his bottle of water to give them a little sip instead. Sometimes those seemingly meaningless choices matter, maybe not for him, but definitely for those thirsty little flowers. He got in his car and was feeling pretty good, all things considered.

Unfortunately, that positive feeling didn't last the whole ride home. He made it a little more than halfway, speeding down the interstate, when his radio stuttered and then went silent. "Seriously," David grumbled, "You've got to be kidding me." He resorted to his first line of troubleshooting electronics.

He smacked the dashboard.

"Come on!" A little flicker of sound came from the speakers. Eyes widened, surprised it had an effect. He did it again. Suddenly, the music crackled and then started back, blaring from his speakers.

"Nothing to it," he said with a smile.

However, as fate would have it, this second smack and the subsequent rush of sound distracted David for just long enough that he didn't notice the truck merging directly into his lane. The moment his eyes looked up from the radio, the front driver's side of his car was hit by a large 18-wheeler that didn't see his little car while changing lanes, causing him to lose control.

The crunch of the impact pushed the front end of the car to the right. He tried to turn to avoid going under the large trailer but overcompensated by trying to stay on the road. He lost control and was sent careening at an uncontrollable speed through the breakdown lane, sliding down the embankment. He hit the brakes, but that only caused the car to start turning sideways. It then flipped a few times and finally came to a stop on the driver's side after slamming into a tree.

The last thing David remembered was the sharp pain throbbing down his left side. Then, everything went black.

5

Dammit.

I complain about being bored, and then this? Not the excitement I was hoping for. A tropical vacation, skydiving, some dangerous new hobby...hell, I would've settled for a wildly unstable girlfriend. But a painful, possibly fatal car accident?

God has quite a dark sense of humor.

And I am not ready for his story to end. Not with him alone, the way he has been for so long. I know I could have done so much more to guide David to happiness, and just hope I get another chance.

As much as my first instinct is typically to panic, I know I have a job to do. And as emotionally painful as it is for me, I know that it pales in comparison to the physical pain David is feeling right now. Having to record all the details of the crash was heartbreaking enough. I knew the accident was bad, but once he lost consciousness, I was put in the dark too. I probably should've paid a little more attention during those classes.

I knew that there were a couple of scenarios that might play out. Either he was going to be moving on to the afterlife, and I would have to start wrapping things up here and preparing the library for David to take ownership, or he was going to be unconscious for some unknown amount of time. Either way, I couldn't just sit on my hands and hope for the best. I put down my pencil and made my way to the spot where he would be showing up if he survived the crash. I grabbed the "average day" book that I kept around. I thought it might buy me some time tonight.

I put the book on the table in front of the couch and waited just around the corner from the last bookshelves. After what felt like an eternity, he was there, lying motionless on the couch, eyes closed. I knew that it meant he was hurt pretty badly, but thankfully, still among the living. I breathed a sigh of relief and felt a small spark of hope. I held on to that feeling tightly while making a silent promise that I would do everything I could to help, as limited as that may be.

As I slowly walked back to my desk, passing the thousands of books on the shelves, I realized how much I had been failing him. A feeling of guilt overtook me, but I couldn't focus on my self-pity. There was plenty of time for that later.

David was alive, at least for now, and I might have an opportunity to make things right.

6

David opened his eyes and found himself lying on a buttery-soft couch. His head was filled with storm clouds, and thunder was pounding against his skull like he was waking up from a wild night of heavy drinking. He lay there for a minute and tried to adjust to his strange surroundings. He began to wonder what the hell he had gotten into, but the memories felt just out of reach. He had been a bit of a partier when he was in his 20s, but those days were long gone. If he *had* been drinking, whose couch did he just wake up on? He tried retracing his steps. He remembered going to work. He remembered getting invited out but staying late in the office to avoid the awkward social interactions. But everything after that was a complete blur. Did he decide to go out after all? Did he get absolutely hammered and go home with someone? He sat up and rubbed his eyes, trying to bring the world into focus. He needed coffee. A lot of it. And something for his absolutely brutal headache.

He looked around. There were end tables on each side of the couch, both covered with a colorful assortment of magazines. There were shelves upon shelves of books in every direction, but it didn't look like any library he could remember. There was a muted, yellowish light above each bookshelf, but he couldn't tell where it was coming from. There were no lamps or candles or anything else that he could see. But somehow, everything about this place felt vaguely familiar.

It was a surreal feeling...like he was awake in a dream. Everything around him seemed just a bit...off. He couldn't put his finger on what exactly made it that way.

Where the hell am I? he thought.

The couch he was sitting on was made of soft, chocolate brown leather and he found it so comfortable that he didn't want to ever get off of it. The coffee table in front of him was a glossy, dark wood matching the bookshelves. The only thing on it was one plain, boring brown leather-bound book. It looked the same as all the books on the shelves around the room. David picked it up and noticed how it seemed brand new. He flipped it over as he looked for a title or a name or anything else that might identify its contents. All he saw were the numbers 00000. He sat back and opened it up...

7

BOOK 00000

EHHHH—EHHHH—EHHHH—EHHHH—

Damn, David groggily thought, *that was weird*. As far as dreams go, he knew it was an odd one, but he couldn't remember why. He lay there for a moment, trying to grab at any pieces that were still floating around in his head. By the time he reached over to grab his phone, any thought of the strangeness was gone, replaced with his typical morning mental rambling. He stayed in bed for a bit. His mind felt extra foggy. The sound of birds quietly chirping away floated in through his window. A feeling of deja vu washed over him.

At some point, I need to just say screw it and sleep in, he thought as he rolled out of bed and into the shower in what seemed like one fluid motion. He finished up, got dressed, made a pop tart, poured some coffee, and left for work. Mindlessly repeating his monotonous morning routine.

On the drive, he was still feeling off. Every time he began to daydream, he would jolt awake as if suddenly realizing he was still behind the wheel of his car. Not that it mattered during this morning commute. Bumper-to-bumper traffic for an hour meant his mind would wander all over and not have to stay locked down for long. On some mornings, there were times when the traffic was light, and he didn't even realize how close he came to falling completely asleep.

Thank God for rumble strips.

Today wasn't like those days, though. *That dream did a number on me*, he thought. The struggle to remember anything about it would come in waves. All he knew was that his head felt like it was full of cobwebs. He started the ride to work listening to music, hoping some melody would help clear them all out. In what felt like a middle finger from the universe, *Everyday is Exactly the Same* by Nine Inch Nails came on.

He spent the rest of the ride thinking about dreams but in a more general sense. His real life had become so mundane and boring and predictable that he only made it through each day because of the thought that his nightly strolls along the vast ocean of impossibilities were waiting for him at the end. It had even reached a point where fitting in small mental excursions throughout his day was not just commonplace but necessary.

Sometimes, the line between his real life and the one he imagined was so blurred that he had trouble figuring out which one was real. He remembered random nights, not often and thankfully not in a long while when his dreams would bring him to his office, and he would wake up feeling a mix of anger and sadness.

Of all his varied dreams, he hated that that was the one that came true.

It was with that train of thought that he finally arrived at the office. He made sure to stop by the parking lot pavement flowers on his way in. He knew they were real. Nothing that clung that hard to such a tough life could be anything else. But as he made his way to the small crack they called home, they were gone. He looked around, making sure he was following the same path to the front door that he always had. A sudden wave of confusion hit him, and his mind tumbled into another feeling.

Deja vu. Again.

He shook his head and quickly realized that anyone watching him right now might start questioning his sanity. He made a beeline for the front door. It was as if the rest of the walk to his desk didn't happen because suddenly, he was there, sitting at his desk, logging on for the day. *What in the hell is going on in my head right now?*

Work was a blur. Not because he was busy or anything remotely close to that. It was just one of those days that happened completely unremarkably. Coworkers passed by his cubicle as wordlessly as usual. No emails from his boss thanking him for working late. His silent protest to that perceived slight was a lot more daydreaming. His thoughts seemed random, though. None of the stuff that typically populated his work daydreams. Books…the sudden urge to go couch shopping…and weird bouts of anxiety whenever the thought of driving home crossed his mind. His head was still cloudy, and everything seemed just a little off. He was trying to identify exactly what he was feeling, other than the passing bouts of deja vu. Before he knew it, the time to pack up for the day had arrived.

On the walk to the car, he realized he could finally name the feeling that had been taking momentary holds of his thoughts; Foreboding. *Haven't felt that one in a while.* He got in and had an overwhelming sense of unease as he put his hands on the wheel. He sat there for a minute, trying to put his finger on a thought that was just out of reach. It was like trying to grab hold of smoke.

With all those worries and weird feelings, he drove extra carefully. Fortunately, the ride home proved to be as uneventful as the rest of the day. However, he seemed extra jumpy any time a big truck passed him on the highway. Finally, he pulled slowly into the parking lot of his apartment.

As he walked up the stairs to his door, his thoughts were still disconnected from reality. They were filled with many strange feelings, and none felt logical. The sense of foreboding was beginning to fade, but in its place was a rising anxiety. There was also the deja vu that had come and gone multiple times throughout the day. Couldn't figure that one out either. On top of everything else was a pounding headache and just general soreness that was completely unexplained.

It all felt pretty damn weird.

He popped a couple of Advil and decided the answer to his problems was that he just needed to relax a bit. He threw a pizza in the oven and clicked on his TV. Figured tonight would be a good one to mindlessly turn on a movie and just relax on the couch. He flipped through Netflix for a few before settling on a nature documentary. He didn't watch these to learn anything new. He just loved the visuals. Getting to visit faraway, beautiful places, even if it was only on his TV, made him happy. He longed for the days when he would wake up in the morning and spontaneously go explore some new piece of the nearby world.

During his first couple years after moving up here, he would spend nearly every weekend finding some new trail or mountain or bit of coastline to discover. He missed doing all this with his friends but purposely focused instead on how much he was learning about himself. There were so many layers to everything out there that he hadn't noticed before. When he used to go on hikes down south, it was always about sharing the moments of clean, fresh air and beautiful panoramic views with people he cared about. Even though he was still able to enjoy the smells and views, he fell in love with the sounds while out there on his own. Hearing the wind rustle the leaves in trees or the birds calling out to each other or the waves rushing up to greet the shoreline...it didn't matter where he went; the sounds would get him to an almost meditative state of mind. Each separate setting had its own beautiful soundtrack.

These weekend excursions ended abruptly one random Saturday when he slipped on a rock while crossing a small stream. He twisted his ankle pretty badly and realized he had no one to call for help. He didn't think it was quite serious enough to warrant an ambulance, so he slowly limped the mile back to his car and drove home. He decided then and there that he would pause his solo trips out into nature until he had some friends to come with him. That pause turned into a hard stop. He tried to fight the fear of being alone, but it wasn't always effective. Now, the closest he came to a hike was when he'd take a walk to the apartment's mailboxes.

He finished watching the documentary (this one about the Florida Everglades) and just clicked on the first "recommended for you" option: a true crime documentary about a missing person in South Florida. He passively watched it while playing on his phone. It didn't take long for him to decide to call it a day and get ready for some sleep.

As he lay down in his comfortable bed, he had a slightly less-than-comfortable thought. *If something really bad ever happened to me, how would anyone even know? My nearest family is 1000 miles away. Besides occasional emails, I haven't talked to my closest friends in years. Nobody ever comes to visit.* These thoughts weren't completely foreign to him. Being so far away from everyone he loved meant he had to face some difficult feelings of loneliness at times. But he did well with pushing them aside.

No need to worry about all that right now. I'll give the guys a call tomorrow.

He wished he would anyway. It felt great to hear from his old friends, but he just couldn't reach out himself. He always felt like he was intruding on their happier lives. That part of him, the part that didn't feel like a burden, died when he left all those years ago.

And with that final random thought, he put an end to what had been a pretty weird day. He laid down in bed, pulled the covers close, and closed his eyes, hoping for another pleasant, nostalgia-laced night of dreams.

8

In an instant, the vivid, lucid dream overtook him. He was back in that same strange library-type place from the night before. More than that, though, he was in the same exact spot, holding the same leather-bound book while sitting on the same brown couch. He set the book down on the dark wood table in front of him gently, as if he was trying very carefully not to disturb its contents.

Okay, this is kinda messed up... he thought. He could remember times when the dreams he had would feel similar to each other or have some common theme over multiple days. Typically, those would happen when he had some thought whispering in the back of his mind all day. This felt different. The soft, brown couch, the seemingly endless shelves full of books, it felt like a place he knew somehow, even though he couldn't remember ever dreaming about it before last night. The room reminded him of some dust-covered, long-forgotten basement in a library.

He sat up straight and began looking around, building a small list of things to try and match up with his memories. There didn't seem to be any doors, at least any that he could see from his limited perspective. There was a row of bookshelves forming a nearly complete wall in front of him, with openings on each side. Like everything else here, the walls behind him were covered in books, although these were broken up at certain points with tables strewn with magazines. The books that covered the shelves looked like they were all roughly the same size in varying shades of brown. They looked similar to the one now resting on the coffee table. He couldn't make out any titles from where he was sitting.

He realized that it wasn't just the many neatly shelved books that reminded him of a library. It was so quiet. There didn't seem to be even the slightest sound trickling into his ears. It added to his familiar feeling of being completely alone.

He sat there for a moment, weighing his options. He figured he had three to choose from. He could lay back down and just relax for a bit. Maybe go to sleep and see if he woke up back in his bed. He could go grab another book, or maybe a magazine, and see if this dream was trying to tell him something. Or, he could get up and see what this place was all about. He rationalized that if this was just some oddly vivid dream, he might as well explore it a bit.

Option number three it is.

He slowly lifted himself off the couch, his body feeling like it had been sleeping for far too long. Everything felt distantly sore.

That's a new feeling for a dream, he thought to himself.

He walked slowly to the edge of the first bookshelf in front of the couch and peered around the corner. He couldn't make out where the walls were. It looked as if bookshelves were covering almost every bit of available space. There were a few slightly lighter-colored books on some of the next sets of shelves. He was close enough now that he could see that these books were numbered just like the one on the table. The first book in front of him was "13260". He followed the books to the left and noticed they were in order, with the highest number at the end being "13405". He noticed something else about them now. Some of them had what looked like a small strip of gold just above the number.

Confusion was becoming David's predominant feeling but his curiosity was growing at almost the same rate. He didn't know what was going on here but oddly enough, he didn't feel too anxious about it either. He decided to take a quick mental inventory of what he could discern about this dream:

- He knew that he was in a very strange and expansive room filled with thousands upon thousands of numbered books.
- He knew that the numbered books were in numerical order, and all looked pretty much the same.
- Some of these books had varying lengths of small gold strips on them, just above the numbers.

That summed up the certainties. It all felt so strange, but there was something about this dream that seemed important. It was like his mind was trying to give him a message, but he wasn't seeing it yet.

He was just about to grab a random book off the shelf in front of him when he decided against it. He woke up in his bed the last time he opened a book here, and if the dream was ending whenever he opened one, he could wait. He wanted to do a bit more exploring before waking up to another uneventful day. He looked around for some type of exit sign or directions or map or anything that might steer him towards answers. He looked at the numbers on the books, and with no other direction to go, he decided to follow the lower-numbered books as far as he could. He set off around the first row of bookshelves and saw the next row went all the way to the wall with only a small opening in the middle.

No shortcuts, I guess.

As he made his way down the path, he would glance at the numbers on the nearest books. 12002 on one nearby shelf. 10930 a few rows past. He kept moving forward and started paying more attention to the color of the bindings. Whereas the first couple rows were almost entirely darker shades of brown, with a few randomly placed tan-colored books mixed in, he saw that there were now many more lighter-colored editions. Some entire shelves were shades closer to khaki than chocolate brown. But the books with gold strips were more spaced out, and on some of them, the gold strip was very small, barely the size of one of the numbers.

He passed by one of the side tables, covered haphazardly with magazines. He pushed a couple aside to get a better look at the titles. "Explore Florida!", "Space Travel", "Greatest Sports Moments"...they seemed interesting. The covers looked so damn familiar too. Every picture seemed to spark some distant memory. There were probably a couple dozen different magazines just on this table. David figured he could come back to them later. He was on a mission at the moment.

He wasn't even really looking down the rows of books he passed now except to check the numbers every few aisles. 8021. 5179. 3110. 1513. It felt like a slow, cumbersome countdown. But it seemed like he was getting closer to the place that might help him figure out what this dream meant. Or maybe he would just get to the end and hear his alarm waking him up. That thought gave him a brief, quiet laugh.

This probably happens every morning just before that super-annoying alarm starts up. My body is so used to it now that even my dreams have a built-in timer. I swear if I get to the first book and then wake up, I'm going to be pissed, he thought.

His pace began to slow down as he got to the last row of shelves. He could see the slight curvature of the wall behind them. He noticed something else now. There was an odd flicker of light, like that of a candle, bouncing off the shelves. The shadows indicated it was coming from just around the corner.

Something else was coming from that direction, too. David heard a faint noise and immediately froze. It was the first break from the complete silence he had been experiencing. He closed his eyes, trying to focus everything on what it might be. It wasn't loud, but it was familiar—a soft, morse code-like scratching sound.

It sounded like a pencil on paper.

It was then that he realized he had been mistaken. He was not alone in this dream. That was the sound of someone writing.

9

I knew David had been making his way toward me. I had hoped he would wake up by now. I wasn't completely sure I was ready for him to meet me and I had no idea how I was going to even begin explaining what was going on. At the very least, I wanted to have some answers about the accident to share. However, all I knew for certain at this point was that I didn't know much. The small bits and pieces of information I was getting didn't look very good.

Given the situation, I knew there were some rules I might be allowed to break—or at least bend a little. This was a special circumstance, after all. Assuming I had some leeway meant there were some lessons I could finally teach him. There was still no telling what would come next for David or me, so I decided to take it slow. From the information I had been gathering, there was no rush.

For the first time, I would have his full, undivided attention.

I was surprisingly nervous about this. I have been around for David's entire life and know everything about him. But I was about to play a role I never really planned for. I wouldn't just be a voice in his head. Describing what I really am would take some very delicate wording. How do you tell someone that you have been recording their every waking moment while also trying to guide them correctly, and, oh yeah, I'm some guy that died a couple hundred years ago?

The answer: you don't. Not immediately, anyway.

My own experience finding out about Peter after my death was not exactly a joyous celebration. There's always a small amount of time after dying to get used to the afterlife. So after a couple of weeks of seeing loved ones and learning what heaven was like, I was suddenly hit with the news that my every waking moment was journaled! There were plenty of times that I embarrassed myself one way or the other and only shook off that terrible feeling by reassuring myself that no one was around to witness it.

Wrong!

On the plus side, no one has access to your library without being invited. And your conscience is not allowed to speak about your life without your permission.

But enough about me, let's get back to David. I could see his shadow on the far wall, dancing with the light from the flickering flame of a candle on my desk. I just needed a little more time to finish up...

10

David slowly peered around the last of the bookshelves. The wall on the other side was no different, but a dark, wooden desk was nestled snuggly between the shelves. Seated at the dark, wooden desk was an old man, head down, focused intently on the open book in front of him, his pencil dancing across the pages. He had thinning, gray-white hair barely covering the top of his head and a long, white beard. He had on thick, black-rimmed glasses that seemed just a little too large for his narrow face. To add to this odd sight, it looked like he was wearing an old Rage Against the Machine t-shirt.

David thought his brain had given up. White flags were waved.

He stood there, motionless. Of all the dreams he's remembered having, none had been anywhere near this bizarre. Sure, some were strange, but this had now crossed over into feeling completely foreign. He felt like he was pulling back the curtain in Oz like he wasn't supposed to be seeing any of this. There was a war raging inside him. Curiosity was fighting against his fear of intruding somewhere he wasn't supposed to be. Right now, the fear was winning, and he began thinking of escape plans.

The old man continued writing furiously, seemingly oblivious to the fact that he was no longer alone. David thought he should just go quietly back to the couch he had woken up on. *Maybe I'll lay back down, pick up that book again, and wake up in my bed.* That thought gave him a momentary sense of peace. Of all the possible scenarios that were busily playing out in his head, that was the only one that seemed like a rational thought. His dreams were his own, and he didn't want to share them with anyone else. He had just started to quietly turn around and head back when the old man spoke.

"Hello, David," came a soft and raspy but somewhat familiar voice from behind the desk. The old man had noticed him. And he knew his name.

Nope, David thought, *not happening*. Fight or flight kicked in, and David turned and bolted. He couldn't remember the last time he made his body do anything, even a little strenuous. But now, whether it was the adrenaline or something else, he was moving faster than he ever had before, trying to get as much space between him and the old man as he could.

He ran between bookshelves down one of the aisles, finally stopping to listen for footsteps. He could hear them coming, not at a run but at a slow, steady pace. "I just want to wake up, back in my bed," he whispered, hoping his mind would hear the words and magically make it happen.

Then he remembered the book from last night and how opening it seemed to end the dream. He grabbed one off the nearest shelf and, as the footsteps seemed to be getting closer, opened it.

11

Great.

    I figured he might be a little spooked but hoped he would at least give me a few minutes to try and explain things. But, as I probably should've known, he got the hell out of here as quick as his feet would take him. And now, he's off reliving some completely random, unremarkable day from his mid-twenties, and who knows what other memories this trip will spark. Hopefully, I can talk him out of taking more random trips down memory lane until I have a chance to explain things.

    And there are some places I don't think he should go for his own sake.

    It would be just my luck for him to go spend a day doing things with people who bring back a trauma that I went through a lot of trouble to keep hidden.

    Don't judge. David would not have been able to survive any other way. Or maybe he could have, but it would have been way more painful. So, I found a loophole in the rules and have protected him from ever having to think about it again.

There. My short confessional. Now more pressing and complicated, issues need to be focused on.

When he gets back, he will have even more questions for me. The only positive aspect of this is that I might have the time I need to get more concrete answers about what's happening in the real world.

12

BOOK 8407

The sunlight snuck through a small opening between the dark curtains. The warmth caressed Dave's bare back, gently welcoming him to a new day. He rolled over and opened his eyes, looking up at the slowly spinning fan. A smile snuck onto his face as he stretched his arms and legs as far as they would go.

Then, a short burst of confusion hit. *Where am I?*

His room, the same room he'd lived in the last couple of years, felt foreign, distant. He chalked it up to his previous night's activities. *Man, Bobby must've had some good weed*, he thought; *my dreams were seriously crazy.* Try as he might, though, nothing about them was coming back to him. Just blankness and the feeling that they were way out there.

He sat up in his bed, and another strange feeling came out of nowhere: an intense bout of deja vu. He was sure this was something he had experienced before. As soon as he tried to delve into his mind and figure it out, the feeling and associated thoughts exited stage right.

Poof.

He stumbled his way out of the room, remembering the guys were both working. Thoughts and memories felt like they were coming slower than usual, dripping like molasses into his mind. He, again, figured he probably smoked a bit too much the night before. He set about making some strong, black coffee to try and jump-start things a bit.

Sharing an apartment with his best friends had been just as awesome as they always thought it would be. None of them had settled into a career yet, although Jimmy was making good money as an electrician at his dad's company. Dave and Drew both worked a couple of jobs, but nothing that felt like more than just a way to make some spending money. Since graduation, Dave was bouncing between temp jobs, the current one in an accounting office. He couldn't stand being so isolated in a cubicle and kept a few shifts as a bartender at a local dive just to keep his sanity. Drew was trying to break into the culinary field. His days were divided between prep work at a fancy restaurant downtown and being a line cook at the same dive bar where Dave mixed drinks.

They were living the perfect twenty-something bachelor life.

Dave spent the morning doing a whole lot of nothing. With his friends and his girlfriend all working, and the storms outside, he didn't have many options anyway. He ended up mindlessly watching some bad daytime TV.

After a dreamless nap, he figured it was time to start getting ready for work. With the weather being as bad as it was, he knew the bar would be dead, but it was pointless to call out. What the hell else was he doing today anyway? At least he could chill with Drew, and Vanessa had promised to swing by after she finished up at her job. She started working at a small boutique a couple of months ago while going to night school for a business degree. He loved how she seemed to have life already figured out, effortlessly weaving friends, family, work, and school into a beautiful tapestry. He felt lucky to be one of the threads. He sent her a quick text to ask if she was bringing her friend, Katie, to the bar tonight. Drew kept asking about her, and Dave decided to proactively try to set them up.

Typically, the bar would be at least half full on a Saturday night. On a good night, the place would be packed, people standing shoulder to shoulder, trying to get Dave's attention for another round. He loved it, and not just because these were the nights that made his rent. Being around so many people, everyone having a good time, friends stopping by...Dave couldn't get enough of it. As much as the new cubicle life drained his usually high levels of happiness, one night behind the bar gave it all back. Plus, Vanessa usually tried to hang out as much as she could. The best part was that no two nights were ever the same.

The rain pelted him as he ran to his car, thunder crashing in the distance. It was as if the sky had decided it didn't want to be sky anymore. It wanted to be the ocean, but gravity wouldn't allow it to change for long. He drove slowly, barely able to make out the road in front of him through the thick walls of water.

Even though he knew the money would suck tonight, he was just happy to be out of the apartment. He didn't do well with downtime, especially by himself. He often thought about how many hours were wasted just doing nothing, that there were too many experiences always happening, and there was no reason for him not to find them. Fortunately, days like today were rare, and he didn't beat himself up too much about it.

As he pulled into the parking lot, he saw it was pretty much empty. Just a few cars that he recognized as being his coworkers'. There were a handful of regulars that always seemed to be there, usually blending into the background until needing another drink. The storms were bad enough that not even those fixtures were there. Dave walked in to see one guy at the end of the bar and an older couple a little ways away. At least Drew was working so he knew he would have someone to share in his boredom. He headed behind the bar and grabbed some paper towels to try and dry off. Drew's unmissable black mohawk popped up as his friend peered through the window separating the kitchen from the bar.

"Man, did you swim here or something?" he asked, leaning forward and resting his arms on the window opening.

"Felt like it! It's coming down in sheets out there," Dave responded as he was wringing the water out of his shirt. "Should've brought a change of clothes. I won't dry up until I get home. At least it's not busy, so we can get out of here on time."

"Damn right. You'll still be out before me, though. You know us back of the house folks gotta stick around late on Saturdays for extra cleaning," he said as he rolled his eyes.

"Don't act like you're not just going to smoke a joint and make some crazy munchie food combination back there later," Dave laughed.

"Well shit, man, if I'm here late, I'm at least going to make it enjoyable," Drew said. "Vanessa still coming by after work?"

"You're only asking to see if she's bringing Katie," he said.

"Who? Don't even know what you're talking about," the smile on Drew's face gave away his sarcasm.

"Yea, yea…I may have already asked 'Nessa to put in a good word for you," Dave was seriously hoping they would hit it off. Katie was Vanessa's best friend and had just gotten back from a few months in Europe.

"What'd you say?" he asked.

"Just that you wanted to chill with Katie some time but dude, she already knew what was up. I think her exact response was, 'Well, duh'," he said.

"Damn, man, is it that obvious?" Drew asked with a laugh.

Dave just rolled his eyes.

Drew seemed to switch gears after hearing that. "Much appreciated, man. Yo, how about a shot to get the night going? Doesn't exactly look like we're going to need to be on our 'A' game with this crowd."

"Why the hell not, man? You know I don't need an excuse," he laughed.

After the shots and more talking, Drew headed back to the kitchen to whip up some dinners for them. Dave grabbed a book from under the bar that a customer had left behind. He didn't give himself much time to read, so took this opportunity to get a chapter or two in. It seemed interesting. He wasn't sure what it was about, but the title was *Galapagos,* and it was by Kurt Vonnegut. Figured it had to be good.

He barely got through the first chapter when he heard Vanessa's sweet voice.

"Hey, handsome. " Her words always tasted like sugar to his ears.

"Hey, gorgeous," he responded, "Just you tonight?"

"Katie said there was no way she was coming out in this weather. Don't look so disappointed!" She laughed.

"I'm not disappointed, but you know someone who will be," he said.

"Oh well, he should be happy. She said I can give him her number. So now, it's up to him," she said.

"Good! She coming to the beach tomorrow with us?" he asked.

"Yeppers. Drew and Jimmy both coming too?" she asked in response.

"Uh-huh, and I think Jimmy's brother Bobby might come too. You met him about a month ago. He's a cool guy, just always traveling," In reality, nobody knew what he did while he was away. He had an old van that he lived in and just drove around the country, randomly showing up back here, usually with some strangely named weed.

No one complained about that.

"Oh, I remember him. He's an interesting guy," she said with a laugh. It must be cool to just drive around the country, totally free. I couldn't go without a hot shower every day, but more power to him."

"Totally agree. It feels like he's the only one with this whole life thing figured out. At least for himself," Dave said.

"Seems like you have a pretty good idea about it, too, babe," she said. Dave wasn't so sure, though.

"I mean to be honest, I don't know, it just feels like I'm spinning my wheels sometimes. Like I know I can do so much more than I am right now," he explained.

"Well, what can you do to fix that?" She asked.

He thought for a moment before responding.

"I feel like things are just good enough for me not to have to try. Like maybe I need to go somewhere new, try something else. With you, of course. Definitely happy about that part of my life," he laughed nervously.

"Nice recovery," she rolled her eyes, "but seriously, are you saying you'd want to leave here, leave your friends?"

"I don't think I could ever really do that. Not far from them, anyway. I just feel like I need some radical change to happen," he explained.

Now it was her turn to think for a moment before responding. "I think the best way to explain it is that you are looking up at a mountain, right? And the person you want to be is on the top of it, and every day you climb a little higher to get closer to being him. It's like the little steps you take to get there that matter. Sometimes you stumble and fall a little bit, but when you have people who care about you around, they can catch you and get you right back on the climb."

"You think I'm making that climb now, working temp jobs and mixing drinks?" He looked genuinely confused.

"Babe, you may not see it, but I do. You are working two jobs, saving money, and having fun, and so what if you aren't in your career yet? You will be. You just have to trust that it will all work out. I know it will," she said reassuringly.

He knew she was right. She was great at talking him off the ledge. Just another aspect of her character that he was completely in love with.

"I know you're right. I just wish it would happen sooner. I'm so ready just to be wherever it is I'm supposed to be," he told her.

"Don't rush it, babe. Just enjoy the ride," she said, pulling him closer for a kiss. Now, not to give you a pep talk and then leave, but I have to get home. I promised my parents I'd bring them to the airport early tomorrow, and I am not looking forward to that alarm clock."

"Aw, bummer. I was kinda hoping you were spending the night," Dave said with a guilty smile.

"Well...I have some errands to run before the beach. But was kinda planning on staying over tomorrow night if that's okay with you, of course," she said slyly.

"Yeah, definitely," Dave tried unsuccessfully to hide his grin.

"You are too cute! Can't wait to see you in the morning!" She told him as she pulled him in for one more kiss.

Drew peeked his head around the corner from the kitchen. "What about me?"

"You too, punk! Katie's going to come too, so you had better be on your best behavior," she told him.

Dave was always on a high after spending time with Vanessa. He felt so damn lucky to have found her. He practically floated through the last hour of work before finally getting to close things up for the night. The acrid smell of weed smoke began emanating from the kitchen. Dave swung in to take a quick puff with Drew and then headed out.

The drive home felt...odd. The storms had mostly passed, leaving only slick, shiny roads and distant, brief flashes of lightning in the distance. The feeling of deja vu that had been kept at bay while he was working was coming back, but his mind had trouble following along. Trains of thought weren't just leaving the tracks; they were disappearing completely from existence. He turned up his music and focused instead on the plans for tomorrow.

Going to be a kick-ass beach day, he thought.

It wasn't often that his best friends and his girlfriend had the same day off, and the weather was supposed to be perfect. Dave loved it when they all went to the beach as a big group, drinking the whole day and coming back home burned but content after watching the sun set.

Those were the days that felt the most well-lived.

Finally returning to the apartment, Dave was ready to call it a night. He got ready for bed, thinking again about how lucky he was to have a girlfriend like Vanessa. He lay down and thought about how the day had turned out pretty well, even if it had been a little weird at times. He began drifting off to sleep, excited for the morning.

13

When he opened his eyes, he was immediately overwhelmed by confusion. Expecting to wake up in the apartment he shared with his friends, he found himself instead in a dimly lit library on a soft leather couch.

What the hell?

The events of the last couple of days started coming back to him in a slow drip of realizations. He wasn't in his twenties anymore. He hadn't seen his friends in over a decade. He lived far away from them, and the old life that he just dreamt about was part of his distant past.

Or maybe this was the dream?

He sat up and tried to figure out what the hell could possibly be going on here. He remembered being in this place the last few nights. Walking down the aisles of bookshelves, following the trail of numbers on the books, shiny gold strips that seemed randomly placed on some of them, and then the old man…

Damn. Just the thought of that out-of-place, white-bearded man who knew his name writing at some equally out-of-place wooden desk had spooked him again.

Everything he was experiencing was detrimental to his sense of reality. The books, the library, and being back with his friends were indistinguishable from his waking life, except that he knew it couldn't all be real.

This time, he couldn't stop his mouth from saying the words out loud.

"What the actual hell is happening."

Questions were piling up in his brain. He needed to start getting some answers before they blocked his ability to form coherent thoughts. What is this place? Why does it feel like I just lived a day that happened so long ago? Who was that strange old man? However, one particular mystery was rising above the others, and he couldn't figure out why. He had an awesome, beautiful, fun girlfriend but hadn't thought of her in as long as he could remember. It was like she had stopped existing in his memories. Why couldn't he remember anything about what happened in that relationship? She was definitely real and definitely his girlfriend, a serious one, but all that his mind could muster was that she was in his life for a few years, then she wasn't. What was even crazier was that before opening that book, he wouldn't have believed she even existed, like she was part of some hallucinated, hollow memory. He couldn't quite put his finger on it, but the thought of her stirred some intense, conflicting emotions, love and emptiness.

Did she break up with me? Is that what drove me to move away? I feel like I should remember something more about her and us...

Nothing.

He decided to move past that fruitless tree for now and try to figure out what questions he could answer. He went to set the book down on the coffee table in front of him when something shiny caught his eye. The small gold strip he noticed on some of the books was completely across the binding now. He knew for sure it wasn't like that when he originally picked it up. Those strips seemed to glow when he walked down the aisles. The whole reason he grabbed that particular book off of that particular shelf in that particular aisle was that he was trying to hide from the old man, and the darkness felt safe.

As much as he wanted to curl up in a ball, find somewhere else to hide, and wait until he woke back up in his normal, boring life, his need for answers was growing too strong. Not sure if it was a good idea yet, he knew there was something he could do that might help him get some answers.

He had to put his anxiety to rest for a moment and find the old man.

Quietly, clutching the book in his hand almost like a weapon, he got off the couch and began walking back to the spot where he had seen him before. This time, the only thing he was looking for when peering down the aisles was the glowing gold strips on the books. He noted that although they seemed random and lacked any discernible pattern, some aspects of their placement struck him as possibly important or, at the very least, meaningful. There were many books with very small strips, barely the thickness of his pinky, spread out over the first couple of aisles he walked by. As he walked on, there were fewer and fewer, but the ones he did see were larger and brighter. A couple stretched nearly across the whole binding, just a little smaller than the one on the book he was still holding. He had no idea what this meant, if anything at all. He decided that it was something he could find out about after the bigger question of 'what the hell was going on' was finally answered.

A few more aisles, and he could start to see the bouncing of the candlelight shadows. He knew the old man's desk was right around the corner. He could hear the same sounds of pencil on paper and knew it had to mean he was writing again.

David stood there, at the precipice between knowing and not. The light from the old man's desk was just in front of him, and he hesitated to cross it. He took a deep breath and then slowly stepped forward.

14

After checking on the book David had opened, I knew a new problem was about to arise, one that I had hoped to avoid above all others. There would be questions about Vanessa, and I'm not sure yet how exactly to walk that fine line between being honest and protecting him.

Hopefully, I can keep him focused on the more present, serious issues, like why he's even here and what that means.

I guess only time will tell.

Unfortunately, I have very few solid facts to share about his current physical condition. The news on that front is still very much up in the air. I must...

Delay, delay, delay.

I know that he is currently making his way back to my desk. His thirst for answers continues to grow. I have some ideas on how to quench it without giving away too much, but none inspire confidence.

I still need more time, but I'm unsure how much I really have...

15

David moved out of the shadows, and the old man finally came into view. His appearance was the same as before: slightly disheveled, with thick glasses and a long beard. He was hunched over the desk, intensely focused on whatever he was writing. He had not yet seemed to notice David was there.

Through a growing nervousness, David went to speak first this time.

He ran into a problem, though. He tried to find his voice, but it felt like he had forgotten how to speak. It was like all the thoughts living in his head were fighting to get out, but the door was jammed shut. He took a few slow steps toward the old man's desk and tried to clear his throat, looking for some way to get the words to spill out.

When he was finally able to open his mouth, he said this:

"Hey."

His voice felt wrong. Or not really there. He didn't know how to describe the feeling. He knew a word had just left his lips, but it didn't feel like there was ever one there to begin with. An emptily uttered syllable.

It wasn't much of a loquacious start to the conversation anyway. Oddly, the old man held up a finger, telling David to wait. He obviously had to finish his work before he could do anything else.

This did not help David's nerves.

The old man finally put down his pencil, looked up, smiled, and waved David over to a comfortable brown leather chair next to the desk.

David sat down but still couldn't find the right combination of words that wanted to leave his mouth. He gave an awkward nod that he was sure looked about as uncomfortable as it felt. *God, just relax, man,* he thought to himself. He wasn't sure why he was feeling so damn nervous in his dream.

Then the old man spoke. "I'm sure your mind is absolutely swimming in deep questions and hypothetical scenarios right now. Let me start by letting you know that this is a safe place, and you have nothing to fear. So please, don't go running off again, at least until you let me explain a few things."

"Okay," came David's weak response, feeling a little ashamed at having a frail-looking old man freak him out to the point of running full speed away from him. "Got it. Sorry about that. Nothing to fear…but you're right, I do have a ton of questions…"

"As you should!" the old man practically shouted. "I would be somewhat worried if you arrived and already knew everything! But before we get to all that, and trust me, I will give you as much information as I can, I feel like I should introduce myself. My name is Matthew, and it is a pleasure to finally meet you."

David was still trying to piece things together but decided to see where this was all going. "It's…it's nice to meet you too, Matthew. Look, I've got to ask, what is this place? I thought it was a dream but I'm seriously doubting myself right now. I felt like I just lived a day that I know happened over a decade ago, and I know that's not possible."

Matthew's eyes got larger, but his soft smile remained. "Ahh, what you believe to be possible might be somewhat limited. And you start with the big question right off the bat. I expected nothing less. Unfortunately, that's a very hard one to properly answer at the moment. I can tell you that your assessment of this being a dream isn't very far off, though. But why don't we start with some smaller questions, and we can build ourselves back up to that one? I'm sure you have plenty more you're wondering about."

David thought for a moment. So many questions about what was happening right now. The moment seemed to stretch uncomfortably long. The old man was patient, though. Finally, David responded, "OK. Who are you? Your voice seems kind of familiar, but I can't quite place where I know you from."

"I am..." Matthew started to say before pausing. "Well, I guess that is a bit harder to answer than I anticipated." He couldn't help but let out a small laugh.

He continued. "I think the best way to explain it, for now, is I am that voice in your head that tries to steer you in the right direction."

Matthew was looking to David for his reaction, and seeing only more confusion wash over his face, he pressed on. "I may seem familiar because you've heard my voice throughout your life. It may come as a surprise, but there have been times when we've conversed before this moment, though not in the same way you talk to people in your regular life or even the way we are now. Think back to when you've tried to figure out some decision and gone back and forth attempting to weigh all possible outcomes. That was us. You, of course, saw these moments as just an inner dialogue, which, again, isn't very far off from the truth."

David's mind raced, but he followed along as best he could. "Like when I would want to quit my job and quickly decide that wasn't a good idea?"

"Yes, that is a good, recent example. When you have wanted to make a rash decision, I have tried to be a voice of reason. Your choices are still your own, and I am not infallible but I have tried to help you when possible. Not that you've always listened to my advice." This was starting to blow David's mind. The questions were all bubbling over now.

"Is this the same for everyone? Am I the only one with a...' Matthew' in my head?" he wondered out loud.

"Let's start with the fact that I'm not living in your head. Everyone has an inner voice of reason or conscience or guardian angel. There are many names for it. Some people have stronger inner voices; some are quieter. There is no one-size-fits-all version since no two people are the same." Matthew was speaking in an even, matter-of-fact tone. David was trying to wrap his head around the idea that not only was he sitting across from his conscience, but that he was the first 'person' David had spoken to, for more than just a few words, in years. And he wasn't even real. No matter how depressing that thought was, he wanted to focus on finding as much information as possible. Something still felt off, though.

"I know you said we've talked before, but have we ever met? It's more than just your voice that feels familiar," David wondered.

"That would depend on how you define 'met'. I've popped into your dreams from time to time when you've needed a little guidance. That has been the extent of it, though, and the only thing you would likely remember about those encounters is waking up with a little more insight or direction on a particular issue," Matthew explained.

That stirred a follow-up question from David, "Wait, do you control my dreams?"

"No, although I may try, not always successfully, to give them some type of purpose, your dreamworld is a fantastical place that your mind creates every night and then cleans out each morning. You sometimes remember bits and pieces of the best parts, but time works differently there. For example, when you wake up thinking that you've dreamt of the beaches you grew up near, that would only be a small fraction of everything you did in your dream." Matthew knew it was all so much more complex than that, but now was not the time to delve into the inner mechanics of dreams. He wanted to keep things moving along.

David, however, was completely fascinated by this aspect. He knew from those terribly early mornings when he hit the snooze button on his alarm that 8 minutes could feel much, much longer. But he never really pieced together what that meant for all the other hours that preceded the alarm. He realized there was so much about himself he didn't even know—or at least that he didn't fully remember.

He wondered if this dream would also follow that pattern. Would he randomly wake up at some point and only remember that there was something about books and an odd old man?

"Is that what's happening now? Am I about to wake up and not remember anything except having some strange dream?" he asked.

"Well, you have plenty of time to explore this dream, if that's your worry. And it is not impossible to know ahead of time how much you will remember," Matthew responded.

"Can I just have a minute to think about this? My head feels overloaded. " David hoped his understanding would catch up to the situation, but he wasn't feeling very optimistic.

"Of course! Take all the time you need. I don't have anywhere else to be," Matthew answered and smiled.

David tried to understand all of this new information, but it was like his head was an old computer with years of neglect being asked to run some incredibly complex program. He could almost see a warning message pop up, telling him there was insufficient processing power. Fortunately, Matthew gave him time to think without rushing him to a quicker but insufficient understanding.

There was a lot to take in. First off, he had a conscience. Well, that part wasn't a complete shock. He had always assumed that most decent people had one. But to see him as a person and talk to him was a bit much. Not only that, but Matthew had also been there, guiding him through times when difficult choices were made. David could feel a creeping sense of frustration and resentment as he thought about where all his decisions had taken him.

His brain had finally rebooted, and he thought he heard the old Windows 95 start-up sounds coming from somewhere. He decided to ask him about the hard path he took in life. "So, backtrack for a second. If you had been the one who helped me when I had to decide something big, why does it seem like I made the wrong choice so many times?"

Matthew knew this question might come up but still wasn't completely ready for it. He absentmindedly stroked his beard while carefully choosing his words before responding. "It is true that I tried to guide you through your most difficult choices. However, those choices were still completely yours. As much as I wanted to shield you from any pain, I could not make you choose the path I wanted you to walk. You had to choose it yourself. And there were many times when you shut me out completely. And, honestly, that was okay. Everyone goes through times when they make decisions quickly, only to regret them later. That is a part of life. Sometimes those painful lessons are the ones that bring the most understanding."

David thought about this for a moment. He knew Matthew was right. He remembered the years after first becoming an adult when every decision he made seemed to go wrong. He was so sure of himself back then that it didn't matter who was telling him something was a bad idea. If he wanted to do it, he would do it. He operated on a dangerous combination of spontaneity and a damn-the-consequences feeling of invincibility. He felt a sudden pang of remorse.

"Man, I'm sorry I shut you out," David said as he put his head down.

"It is not something you have to apologize for, David. Everyone has a path they must walk down, and sometimes, that path can be treacherous. Your path has led you here. We will have more time to discuss all of those decisions. But for now, why don't we move on to some of those other questions that I'm sure you want to ask," Matthew explained.

As much as he wanted to continue, he decided Matthew was right. He still had so many questions. He looked around the room before settling on the one that got him off the couch in the first place.

"What's up with all the books? And why are all they in numerical order?" he asked.

"I was wondering when you'd get around to asking that," said Matthew. "The books are all tiny slices of one much longer story. Each one is important, but it takes all of them to understand the subject truly."

Is there a cliff notes version? David wondered to himself before saying out loud, "What subject could possibly need thousands upon thousands of books for someone to understand it?"

Matthew thought for a moment. He looked over at the books on his desk and chose one. "Here, take this one. Opening it should provide a starting point for the rest of this conversation. You know what they say, 'Experience is the best teacher.'"

That is awfully cryptic, David thought. He wanted to ask why Matthew couldn't just explain things to him but thought better of it. He just finished apologizing for not listening to him. No need to go right back to doing it again so quickly.

"After I opened the last couple of books, I ended up back on the couch. Is that going to happen again?" He asked.

"Yes, and I will be over there, ready to guide you to a greater understanding," Matthew reassured him.

David held the book for a moment. It was dark brown with a stiff leather binding. It had "13407" printed on its spine, with a gold strip just above the number that stretched nearly across the binding. Another question he would have to wait to ask. There was something familiar about all of this, but he couldn't quite put his finger on what exactly it was. He sat back in his chair and opened it slowly.

16
BOOK 13407

EHHHH-EHHHH-EHHHHH-EHH...

David lay there for a moment, head trying to adjust to the world around him. The pillow was soft, and as he rolled over, away from the early morning light peaking through his curtains, he wrapped himself a little tighter with his blanket. It was early spring, and even though the mornings of frost-covered grass were over, there was still plenty of chill in the air. None of this made it any easier to fully leave the comfort of his warm bed. The sounds of nature waking up outside were the only noises David could hear. His ears caught the light-muffled melody of birds singing outside. His apartment was on the third floor of a small apartment complex, and there were a few trees whose top branches were not far from his bedroom window. He loved sleeping with it open just enough to let some of the cold air in at night. Once spring arrived, it had an added benefit. The sounds coming from out there would offer him a gentle auditory contrast to the harshness of his alarm. *That is how everyone should wake up,* he thought, *being gently brought out of sleep by the sounds of the day starting up.* He couldn't remember the last time he got to experience that kind of subtle end to his dreams. Waking up to the loud ringing of an alarm clock was how his mornings always started, and he believed it to be unnatural and not something any sane person could ever get used to. Even after years of enduring this, he never looked at it with anything less than disdain. It was an unfortunate side effect of having to go to work, to pay bills, to survive. David hated all of it.

Wow, he thought. *This is some serious deja vu. Maybe my days are getting so ordinary that I can't tell one from the next anymore.* It was true that all his days had become carbon copies of each other, but he could still tell them apart by his dreams. He realized a long time ago that his dreams had been becoming increasingly the high point of his day, and the struggle to leave them each morning was a growing challenge. Even the dreams he struggled to remember had a way of leaving small little bits of information for him to think about throughout the day, making him long to return to sleep and try to go back. Today felt different, though. His alarm stirred him just enough that he left his dream but not quite enough to be awake. The deja vu he was feeling felt like it had something to do with his dream, but he couldn't remember anything about it. He laid there for a moment, consumed by the desire to close his eyes and try to go back and find some little breadcrumb to follow. *Maybe I could... just for a few more minutes...*

EHHHH-EHHHH-EHHH...

Damn snooze button. Sometimes the time between alarms felt like hours, and he would get great sleep in between those 8 minutes. Not today, though. Even with his mind swimming in a sea of confusion, it seemed to him that the alarms happened almost concurrently. He didn't see any point in delaying the inevitable. Time to start the day. If the dream was that important, he was sure he would have remembered something. But he couldn't shake the feeling that he had these same thoughts before.

He lay there trying to latch on to any fragments of thought but they seemed to fade away the moment he fully opened his eyes. He would have to settle for a few minutes of reaching blindly for a silent, moving target. There was an image, cloudy, out of focus, that he was trying to reach...it was...something about books? It didn't make any sense. With his head struggling to snap back to reality, he decided it was pointless to keep dwelling on it. He grabbed his phone and absentmindedly began his morning scrolling.

Somehow he pulled together enough energy to lift himself out of bed and made it to the shower. This was typically when his brain would finally begin turning on for the day. The hot water always did the trick. The morning fog that clouded his head was starting to get burned off. Not completely but at least enough to think about the day ahead. There would be the usual drive to work. That would be followed by 8 hours of sitting at his desk. Then he drives home before wrapping up his day watching TV. He wasn't even out of the shower yet, and the first thing that made him crack a smile was when the thought of climbing back into his bed tonight crossed his mind.

It was going to be a long day.

He begrudgingly finished up, got dressed, grabbed a pop tart, made some coffee. The same thing he did every morning. He was able to get through all of this on autopilot.

The day passed by like all the others. Unremarkably. He drove to work. He sat at his desk. He daydreamed. He carefully avoided any social interaction beyond the very basic "Good morning, Kathy," or "Take care, Jon," or "Sorry I didn't make it out on Friday, but maybe next time, Tom." There were times that David imagined he could have 5 or 6 prerecorded messages ready to go and get by with just randomly pressing them whenever someone from the office came by. As much as his morning felt scripted, his work time played out more like an intermission for his dreams.

But throughout the day today, he found himself with strong, recurring feelings of deja vu. He always found it interesting, like some major moment was foretold, and now he gets to live it. However, he noticed it was rarely that serious. Usually doing some menial task or walking down a particular street and then asking himself, *why is this so familiar?* Only to answer himself, *oh yeah, I think I had a dream about this*. This was then followed closely by, *no, David, you've just walked down this road before,* or *you just did the dishes yesterday, and of course, it feels the same*. His brain would always find the logical reason something was happening. It kind of took the fun out of the fantasy.

He brushed off the weird feelings anytime they popped up. It wasn't difficult. He spent the day toiling away at his desk. And when he finally finished up his work, he booked it out of there. His car ride home was a blur; before he knew it, he was climbing the stairs to his apartment and could finally relax.

He spent the time while making his dinner, deciding what he was going to do to pass the time before bed. Tonight, he settled on getting lost in a book. He loved the temporary escape from reality, and a good book could transport him to any place he wanted. Tonight, he stretched out on his couch and grabbed a personal favorite from his bookshelf. *Galapagos* by Kurt Vonnegut. David knew the story well and always enjoyed the way the story was told by a ghost, disconnectedly watching the events unfold. He had felt like his life was playing out in a similar way. Viewing his friends and family's lives from a distance on social media, never really interacting but still hoping everything worked out for the best.

When he finished re-reading the first few chapters, he looked up at his clock and noticed it was almost midnight. It was time to go to bed and get lost in his dreams. He made his way to his room and cracked his window a bit. The wind was blowing some fresh, cool air in, and to David, there was no better way to sleep than wrapped up in a blanket in a chilly room. He laid down, closed his eyes, and silently bid adieu to the strange day.

84

17

David opened his eyes. He was lying back on the comfortable, soft leather couch with book 13407 sitting closed on his chest. It felt like he was just waking up from a brief but intensely dream-filled nap. Cutting through the fog in his mind were the facts of what he just did. He just relived a day from earlier this week. Like completely, from the moment he woke up until the moment he fell asleep, he just did everything again. He was starting to understand what was happening, at least about the books here. He wasn't sure how, but they seemed to contain a full day of his life within their pages. Or that's what it felt like after the first few he had opened. The feeling was a bit disorientating but not unpleasant. He glanced over and Matthew was dusting the shelves nearby. Hearing David stir, Matthew turned around, trying to decide if it was a good time to go back to their conversation.

David sat up and Matthew took a seat next to him.

"So, David, did that book help you? Did it answer your question about what these books are?" Matthew asked.

"I think so…" he started. He knew the answers were coming; he just had to remain patient. He trusted that Matthew would steer him in the right direction. "Each of them is a day of my life. When I open one, I go back to that day. Is that right?"

Matthew smiled. "That is correct. Together, they tell the story of your life, broken into manageable daily chunks. They chronicle every moment you've spent awake, from the day you were born to your present life."

"And the numbers…they start from the day I was born, which would be Book 1, right?" David asked.

"That is correct. The day you just visited was the thirteen thousandth, four hundred, and seventh day that you've been alive," Matthew answered.

David looked around the dimly lit room. Every book is a different day in his life. Although the one he had just been holding wasn't very eventful, he was amazed at the attention to detail. It had felt like the first time he had lived it. There was only one thing that seemed different. He remembered the deja vu.

"There were times while I was reliving this one…", David held up 13407, "…where it felt like I had done it before. I know I did do it all before, but how could I have felt it while I was there? How is that possible? I don't remember feeling that the first time I lived it."

"Ah, yes. That feeling you sometimes write off as just deja vu is a minor side effect of reliving a day. Now, not all of those feelings are from opening one of these books; they are completely normal feelings, but they are something you will feel anytime you revisit one. Although every detail is recorded, your mind may focus on different things. And sometimes, you will feel deja vu when a memory crashes into that focus," he explained.

"But how are my days recorded like that? It seriously felt like the first time I lived it. Like every single little detail was there," David said.

"I must humbly confess that I am responsible for tracking every detail. Not a moment is missing in any of them. Every amazing time you've had. Every embarrassing faux pax. The days that seemed hopeless. The days you felt invincible. All here. The exact steps for how I do it are not very important, but I can tell you that these books are special and that I am very meticulous," Matthew's face took on the look of a proud artist, displaying his greatest work for the first time.

Well, I am very proud of my work.

"So that dream I had when I was in my twenties, back in Florida with my friends...that was real? Like it really happened before?" David asked.

"Yes. I wouldn't have advised you to pick a random day from your past to relive, not knowing how to tell the good ones from the difficult," Matthew responded.

This wasn't just another dream. He still didn't know what exactly it was...maybe he was getting a backstage pass to where his dreams were made. If he could just pick and choose different previous experiences, maybe he could at least have some fun before it ended.

"So, if these are stories about every day I've lived, could I just go back and read the parts I wanted to?" David asked. He thought about how great it would be just to go back and experience all the fun he had drinking with his friends, minus the hangovers, or maybe only reliving the parts of certain days that were good, like going out after work or after class.

Matthew responded, "Unfortunately, it doesn't work that way. When you choose to open one of the books here, you will relive that full day from start to finish. Each one begins with the moment you wake up and doesn't end until the time you fall asleep."

Disappointment. But it gave David a new question. "What about my time asleep? Like when I'm dreaming, is all that here too?"

"Yes, your dreams are also kept here, but they can't be found on the pages of the books. I'm sure you've noticed the magazines scattered about. Unfortunately, there is not a good way to organize the random chaos that dreams can bring," Matthew explained.

David remembered seeing all the colorful magazines strewn about on the tables while trying to find the first book. Now he knew why the covers seemed so familiar. He made a mental note to make sure he took a closer look at "Flight" as soon as he could. That one seemed especially enticing.

Matthew spoke. "Here, I have an idea. You just relived a very recent day. Still fresh in your memory. And the random one you chose was pretty average. I think you should go a little farther back to one of your best days. One that you may think you remember perfectly. Spending a day as your younger self might give you a slightly different perspective."

Matthew got up, walked around the table in front of the couch, and motioned for David to follow him. They rounded the corner at the first bookshelf and began walking back in the same direction as Matthew's desk. David looked down the first few aisles, marveling that these thousands of books, taken together, contained the entirety of his life.

The old man turned down an aisle with David following close behind. "I'm sure you've noticed how the books are slightly different hues of brown. There is a reason for that. They are color-coded to represent how 'good' of a day you had. The lighter the binding, the better the day. You've had plenty of darkness in your life, David, but I'm sure you noticed how many of these books are almost completely white."

David had made a mental note of this on that first walk. He recalled how the first few rows of bookshelves in the back of this place were almost entirely dark. But as he walked toward the place where he found the old man, he began seeing more and more lighter-colored books. Entire bookshelves seemed to slowly transition from lighter shades to darker ones and back again, punctuated periodically with very dark or very light editions. He was suddenly curious about how this aspect of it all worked.

"So, who decides how good of a day I had?" David asked inquisitively.

Matthew spoke in a calm, measured tone. "You do, David. It's not something you consciously choose each day, but it's still your choices that determine whether it is good or bad. And as you can see, most days are some combination of both. When you look over these shelves, the variations from day-to-day are mostly subtle."

David thought about that as he looked down the aisle. You had to look at entire bookshelves or rows of them to notice the bigger shifts. There was, however, one particular book that had now caught his eye. He noticed a solid white one practically glowing a couple of shelves away.

"If the lighter the cover, the better the day, does that one mean it was like the best day ever?" David asked as he pointed it out.

"Ah, you must have noticed 4801. It was the first truly great day of your teenage years. You had a couple more, but this one had such a lasting effect on you," The old man reached for it. "This was such an all-around amazing day. It contained so many 'firsts' and was spent at your favorite beach with your best friends. This day is a big reason it became your favorite beach. It was one that you and your closest friends talked about for many years afterward, although the details may have slowly changed with each re-telling." he said with a wink.

David couldn't contain his smile. He remembered this day—not all of it, of course. The decades since it happened wore down some of the memories the way a vinyl record might not hit all of its notes after being played too often. But he remembered enough to know he had wished many times over the years to do what Matthew was now offering him: the chance to relive it.

He tried to keep his excitement in check. But with the huge grin on his face, he was failing. "Matthew, is this really happening? Can I really do that day over again?" David asked, half-expecting him to say he was sorry, but the book was broken, and they would just have to find a different one.

"Of course you can, David," Matthew said with a smile. "I know that this is something you have longed for. I only hope that it lives up to your expectations. And I want you to know that none of these books are off-limits while you are here."

David nodded, unsure if he was speechless because of the completely unreal situation he found himself in or because of his excitement about returning and doing that particular day again. It didn't even matter the reason. David was happier than he could remember being in a very long time.

They made their way back to the couch, David giddily following behind Matthew. He was trying to remember as much as he could about that day on the short walk. He knew it was with his best friends, and he knew it involved the beach. He knew they had a great time and spent the whole day there. Everything else seemed to be a blur. They both sat back down in their seats. The old man handed the book to David.

"Now, just to warn you, when you open this book, you will not remember anything that happened after that day. You've had a small taste of that but this is different. With how much memories naturally fade over time, everything will feel like a new experience for you. Are you sure you're ready?" Matthew asked with a slight smile on his face. He knew that David was about to see firsthand why this day had such a profoundly positive impact on his teenage years.

As much as David wanted to yell, "HELL YEA, I'M READY!!!" He instead simply nodded with a giant smile, barely masking his overflowing excitement.

Matthew passed the book to David, and after a deep breath, he opened it.

18

Once David was off reliving that day, I had work to do. I knew there was precious little time to check in and see if any more of David's real-world senses were working yet. I was getting almost all of my information about what was going on from only his hearing and to say it was a challenge would be a massive understatement. From the little bits of conversation I was able to piece together, the doctors were unsure about his chances. The key phrases that gave me the most fear were "possibly severe brain damage," "paralysis," and "vegetable," although that last one might have been related to a meal someone was having.

Hopefully.

I recorded what I could and began trying to plan for what might come next. I had to try and remember as much as I could from the classes I took before being assigned.

unfortunately, I may not have been fully following along during "Special Circumstances and How to Handle Them."

So, I guess I'm winging it. However, as long as I'm focused on helping David, I'm doing my job. And with how much I felt I had failed him up until this point, I want to help him get through this more than anything.

At the very least, I knew that I could help David remember some great days. Hopefully, this will soften the blow if things take a turn for the worse.

19

BOOK 4801

RRRIIIIIIIINNNNNGGGGG……..RRRIIIIIIIINN NNNGGGGG……...

The phone shook Davy from what had otherwise been a peaceful, deep sleep. He clumsily reached for the football-shaped phone on the nightstand next to his bed. "Hello?" he mumbled.

"DUDE! I know you're not still sleeping!" came a familiar voice. It was Jimmy. He had been his best friend since third grade. They lived on the same street, rode their bikes to school together, and had become like brothers.

Davy looked at the clock. It was 9:00 a.m. He had forgotten to set his alarm—or, more accurately, didn't want to. There was no way he was getting up this early during the summer unless someone forced him to.

"I'm up now, man!" Davy groggily responded. He rubbed his eyes and rolled over onto his back. "When are you coming over?"

"Leaving in like 5 minutes, so get your booty out of bed! BEACH DAY, DUDE!!!" came Jimmy's voice over the phone.

Davy scoffed. "Hell yeah, I'll be ready! I'm getting up now."

"You better be! See you soon, dude!" Jimmy said before hanging up.

Davy flung his covers off and stretched his arms and legs out wide. He felt great. But when he sat up and looked around the room, he felt momentarily out of place. He didn't know why. *Guess I should clean my room when I get home*, he thought. It wasn't exactly dirty, but it was still a total mess. Worn clothes thrown randomly in and around an overflowing hamper. Some maybe-still-clean clothes hanging on the back of the chair in front of his desk. Empty cups taking up space on most open surfaces. But he knew where everything was and never let his room get so bad that his parents would complain. Ever since the ants tried taking over, he became a bit more concerned about the cleanliness.

He was a teenager now but still young enough to hold on to some of his old childish interests. He was planning on a kid's toy purge this summer but wasn't in a big rush. Part of him wasn't ready to close that chapter completely just yet. The coming clash between what he liked and what was considered cool was still in its infancy. The Green Day poster was good but its cool factor was being brought down by the old one on his door of the Power Rangers. Most of his room had this same mix of the things he loved just a couple of years ago and the things that he was just discovering. Some action figures on top of a dresser are beginning to collect dust. His first CD player was in the middle of a bookshelf with a small stack of his growing collection of grunge. There were some LEGOs on the shelf above the stereo and stacks of comic books just below.

He pushed away the strange feelings of deja vu that started as soon as he got out of bed and went to the bathroom for the quickest wake-up shower ever. The sudden burst of hot water always woke him up. He wrapped himself in a towel and headed back to his room to get ready.

The rest of the house was empty and quiet. His mom had to put in some weekend hours at work. His stepdad was away for the weekend on another fishing trip. He was home alone a lot and had become pretty self-sufficient. Over the last couple of years, he learned how to do his own laundry, cook his own meals, and make minor patchwork repairs when something broke. Nothing too complicated, but he was able to stop a leaky faucet and believed that made him a regular handyman. Thankfully, he learned not to mess with anything electrical a long time ago.

The weeks leading up to the end of the school year found Davy and his friends planning out all the details of the "most epic beach day ever." They were all extremely familiar with the beach, having gone together at least a couple of days each month since they first became friends in elementary school. But going without any adult supervision was going to be different. It was an unspoken sign that they were not kids anymore. The first hurdle they had to clear was how to get to the beach without going through the embarrassment of having one of their parents drop them off.

Jimmy's older brother, Bobby, just got his license and, after some light bribery, agreed to give the group of friends a ride. Davy and Jimmy offered to mow the yard, Bobby's most hated chore, all summer long. In return, Bobby would bring them and their friends to the beach at least once weekly. The one condition was that the group of friends had to leave Bobby alone when other high schoolers were around. He was cool but not cool enough to be seen hanging out with a bunch of middle schoolers. Everyone has lines they won't cross.

Davy finished making his bed, threw on his favorite blue-striped swim trunks with a black tank top and sandals, and grabbed the bags he had put together. After all the prep work that went into it, today had no choice but to be awesome. He decided to grab a quick bite to eat since his friends hadn't shown up yet.

Almost on cue, there was banging on his door. "DAVY!!!"

"I'm coming, man!" Davy yelled from his kitchen. He was grabbing a couple pop tarts from his toaster and a soda from his fridge.

Bobby was driving his mom's van. Davy was the last one to be picked up. His best friends were already packed in there: Jimmy sitting shotgun, Drew in the middle row, and Melissa in the back. Davy took the other back seat and threw his stuff on the empty seat beside Drew.

"Buckle up, kiddies!" Bobby said with a smirk. Although he was a few years older than them, they all thought he was the epitome of cool. Decked out in a straw hat, stylish sunglasses, and a brightly colored green and blue Hawaiian shirt, he made them feel cool by proxy.

Jimmy and Drew spent most of the ride talking about girls. Davy and Melissa shared smirks when Drew began talking about how he was going to find a summer girlfriend today.

"I'm totally doin' it! There's going to be a girl at the beach today who's looking for a summer boyfriend. I just need to find her and be like, 'Hey pretty girl, you can stop looking today and just enjoy the whole summer with me,' and she'll be like, 'You are so right,' and then we will go out in the water and watch the sunset while we hold hands," Drew explained in one excited run-on sentence. It was hard to tell if he was serious or not, but the dreamy look on his face let us know he hoped it would happen.

"Do you think a girl is just going to go along with that? Like, how would she know if she even liked you?" Melissa asked.

Drew responded with a purposely goofy look on his face. "What is there not to like?"

Melissa rolled her eyes while the guys laughed. She turned to Davy and said, "You know, that would never work. Girls want to hang out with somebody they like, not just some random person who smiles at them. Well, most girls, anyway."

"I mean, I wouldn't want to spend time with someone that sucks. They'd have to be fun to talk to." Davy explained.

"Right?! And you can't just look at someone and know if they're cool or not!" she said.

"That's why I'm not even worried about girls today. I just want to have a good time at the beach," Davy told her. The guys overheard, though.

"Lame! The beach is where all the girls are, and if you wait too long, all the good ones will already have boyfriends!" More words of wisdom from Drew.

"Dude! I'm a girl, and I can tell you that's not how any of this works! Like at all!" Melissa laughed.

Bobby finally chimed in, "You guys should listen to Mel because you have no idea what you're talking about! But I'd love to see some public embarrassment, so feel free to go with your fool-proof plan, Drew."

The rest of the ride was filled with more talking and laughing and music. Smiles all around.

They pulled into the beach's dusty, sand-covered parking lot. It was already packed! They found a spot not far from the boardwalk that stretched over the dune and unloaded the van. They had a cooler filled with soda (Bobby snuck a few beers from his dad's stash), some sandwiches, backpacks filled with towels, lotion, snacks, a football, a soccer ball, a frisbee, a radio…good planning meant they had everything they needed and were able to get it all in one trip.

They set up in a spot near the top of the dune, just before the tall yellow-green beach grass. This was Davy's preferred part of the beach when it was crowded. You could look in either direction and see the coastline for miles. The cloudless sky touched the water's edge, and the contrasting shades of blue formed a nearly perfect gradient. The sea breeze blew tiny specks of the salty ocean water into Davy's face as the waves crashed onto the beach. Once he kicked off his flip-flops, he could feel the hot sand on his bare feet and was thankful they came early today. Experience taught him that midday sand on a hot, sunny day would be like walking on tiny hot coals, and he'd have to book it to the cooler wet sand near the receding waves.

The friends didn't waste any time, quickly laying out their towels and racing to the water, running until they jumped into the crashing waves. The coolness of it on Davy's already warming skin felt amazing. He jumped into a big wave and then turned, stretching his arms out to his sides, feeling weightless momentarily on his back. He stared into the big blue vastness of the sky, ears muffled by the water just above them. A thought briefly floated past him.

This is what perfect feels like.

A swell came, gently lifting him up, and he quickly flipped back around and swam out to catch up with his friends. They ended up just past the breaking waves. Drew and Jimmy were talking about some girls that were setting up not far from their spot on the beach. However, Davy wasn't paying much attention to what they were talking about. He was too busy trying to hold back his laughter while watching Melissa mocking them silently.

They stayed in the water for hours, body-surfing the waves in and swimming back out to catch another one, stopping to talk about whatever random thoughts popped into their heads, only to get distracted by the next big wave. It wasn't until they started getting hungry that they realized how long they had been out there.

They made their way back to where they had set up. Jimmy and Drew tried to be as cool as possible when they walked past the group of girls, but Davy didn't even notice them. He was talking with Melissa about a movie he had just seen.

"It's got Bruce Willis, and he's this guy who has to save the world, or like help this girl to save the world, but he doesn't want to at first..." he said.

Melissa stopped him there. "Seriously? Do you mean 'The Fifth Element'? I just saw that a week ago! It was so good!"

"No way! You liked it too? Who did you go with? Drew and Jimmy said they wanted to wait and rent it." Davy had a pretty good idea why. *Probably just to pause it when Milla comes out in the white strappy outfit.*

Not that he hadn't thought of that too.

"My dad wanted to see it, so I asked if I could tag along. I didn't think I was going to like it, but it was pretty great!" she said.

They kept talking, exchanging ideas about what happened after the movie ended. Jimmy and Drew walked a little slower, hoping to catch the attention of some of the girls they passed.

The four friends finally made it back to their spot and pulled sandwiches from their bags. Bobby took their arrival as his cue to meet up with some high schoolers who were just showing up.

"You kids don't do anything stupid, alright?" he told the group.

"Sure, *Dad,*" came Jimmy's sarcastic response.

They laid out on the towels, soaking in the sun's bountiful rays. *This is the life,* Davy thought to himself. And it was just as perfect as he hoped it would be. He stared up at the cloudless sky and thought about how he wished every day could be like this. He knew there would at least be plenty more of them this summer.

He had almost fallen asleep when Jimmy and Drew started getting up. "Dude, wanna throw the football around?" Jimmy asked.

Davy saw they were eyeing a few girls not far from them and figured he would be the odd man out. "Nah, I'm good. You guys go ahead. I'm getting back in the water."

He looked over at Melissa, and she looked like she was just waking up too. "Hey, you wanna go back in the water with me?"

"That's all you, Davy," she said with a smile. "I'm going back to my nap."

Davy smiled back, got up, and went down to the water. The crashing waves were rushing up to greet him. He jumped over the first couple and dove under the next ones once the water was closer to his chest. He reached the point where the waves were no longer crashing, just some intermittent swells. Standing up meant the water was around his neck. Now that he was alone, he stretched his arms wide, looking like a buoyant letter "T." The sun was beating down on him, so he closed his eyes and smiled at the sky. He didn't have a care in the world.

After becoming lost in the peacefulness of the gentle rising and falling, he suddenly felt something grab his shoulder and was sure he somehow jumped up out of the water. He hoped his high-pitched yelp was only in his head. As soon as he could breathe again, he turned around and saw Melissa holding in a laugh as well as anyone could.

"Oh my God, D, I'm sorry! I wasn't trying to scare you!" She was somehow able to say this while looking both genuinely concerned and on the verge of another laughing fit at the same time. Davy couldn't be mad at her, though. Although he never told anyone, he had developed a small crush on her over the last few months. He was sure it was just because they were friends and she was the only girl he ever really dared to talk to. But she was pretty and was always nice to everybody and liked the same stuff he did...

"I wasn't scared! I just thought you were a shark or something." Davy felt like this was a valid excuse and forced a small smile now that his heartbeat had begun returning to normal. Or as normal as it could be since he realized he was out in the water all alone with Melissa.

"Yeah, you gotta watch out for those sharks with hands. Those are the worst!" Melissa was treading water but could still send a splash toward Davy.

Davy splashed her back and smiled as he responded. "Ha-ha-ha. Very funny. You know what I mean!"

She stuck her tongue out at him playfully. "I was just coming out here because Jimmy and Drew moved their stuff to sit next to those girls, and they woke me up. I think we might have lost them."

Davy laughed, "That's cool. Wonder if Drew said that whole thing about finding a summer girlfriend to them?"

"I bet they both did!" Melissa was laughing too.

The two friends stayed out there for a little while, talking about other movies they both liked, then about music, school, and families. Time passed slowly, and the conversation came easily. They had pretty much the same likes and dislikes (except that she had already missed school, and Davy wanted a permanent summer vacation). It kept going until it randomly got quiet—not awkwardly, though.

Davy broke the short silence. "Do you know what time it is? Feels like we've been here all day."

"I think it's like late? I didn't bring a watch," Melissa said.

"Obviously," Davy said. "Bet if we stay out here a little longer, we'll end up seeing the sunset. That'd be pretty cool."

Mel and Davy swam out until they could barely touch the bottom. They were out past the point where the waves were breaking. They rose with every small swell of a potential wave, and it gave them a momentary feeling of weightlessness. The sun was getting closer to the horizon and painted the ocean with a dazzling white-orange glow. They slowly drifted closer together until they were almost shoulder to shoulder. Davy looked over at her. *She really is pretty*, he thought.

Suddenly, he was nervous. Their shoulders bumped into each other when the next swell came. He looked at her, and their eyes connected, but neither of them had any sarcastic or playful comments to say. They were the only people in the universe, and nothing else mattered. Without warning, she turned to him, and he decided right then and there that if he didn't kiss her, this completely perfect girl in this completely perfect setting, he would never kiss anyone.

They pulled each other close and kissed. It was clumsy in a way only a first kiss could be. When their lips pulled away from each other, they didn't say a word at first. With their hands held together under the water, they turned back to the sunset. Davy tried hard to contain his smile. His head was floating in the clouds.

He finally regained the ability the speak. "I didn't think that was going to happen today."

Mel gave a little nervous laugh, "I didn't either...I mean, it was kinda cool, though."

"Yea..." Davy didn't know what else to say. His goofy grin was enough, though. Mel playfully splashed him.

"Don't go getting all weird on me now," she laughed.

They stayed in the water for a little longer before swimming back to shore. They could see the guys were waiting for them by their towels. They dried off and sat down. Thankfully it didn't seem like the guys had seen them kiss. Drew and Jimmy began excitedly telling them that they got the girl's phone numbers. Bobby was nowhere to be seen, but they knew he would turn up. His stuff was still here.

They all sat, laughed, talked, and listened to music until Bobby finally showed back up. They reluctantly packed everything and made their way back to the van. Davy and Melissa sat inconspicuously in the back row together but couldn't help exchanging flirty, goofy smiles a few times during the ride. He didn't want it to end.

When they stopped in front of his house, he panicked. He wanted to hug Melissa, but would that be weird? Before he could even start internally freaking out, she unbuckled her seat belt and put her arms around him. It was like she was in his head.

"You should call me tomorrow," she quickly whispered.

Davy's face was etched with a permanent grin as he waved goodbye to his friends and floated up to his door. It was already dark outside, but he barely noticed. His mind was bouncing from one happy thought to another.

He was finally home. *That was the best day ever*, he thought to himself. His mom was doing the dishes when he walked into the kitchen. His face might as well have been a flashing neon sign saying 'ASK ME ABOUT MY DAY.'

"Looks like someone had a good time at the beach," his mom said with a sly smile.

"It was alright," Davy said as only a teenager could.

"That's all, just alright? That look on your face says it was more than alright." His mom was never one to pry, but Davy had a look of euphoria, and she wasn't sure if it was just a great day or drugs.

"We had fun. Jimmy and Drew met some girls. I was in the water for like hours," he said, trying valiantly not to get to the part where he kissed Mel.

"Didn't Melissa go with you guys? You didn't just abandon her, did you?" she asked.

Play it cool, he thought to himself. "No, she was swimming with me for a while..."

His mom picked up on what wasn't being said and gave a big smile. "Well, she is a very nice girl."

"She's cool...I think I'm going to go get ready for bed though. I'm really tired." He felt like he dodged a bullet. He knew his mom liked Mel, but that just added to his worries about telling her. It wasn't like she was his girlfriend or anything.

Not that he was opposed to that idea, but the thought of her as his girlfriend gave him a weird feeling in his stomach. *Is she his girlfriend now? Is that how it works?* He had questions, but he had no one to ask.

It seemed like his mom had all the information she needed, and she didn't press for anymore. "Okay, well, take a shower first. You don't want to get sand all over your bed. And don't forget to put some aloe on that sunburn."

He rolled his eyes. "Yes, mom."

Davy showered, then went to his room and fell back into bed. He could still feel his body moving with the waves. He fell asleep, picturing himself lying on the deck of a ship, holding Mel's hand while they stared up at a star-filled sky. He happily drifted off to a deep sleep.

20

David opened his eyes back in the library. He was still holding the book but unlike the others he had 'read,' he was in no hurry to put this one down. He looked up and saw Matthew, book open in his lap, writing. He took a moment to reflect on what he just got to experience and couldn't help but grin from ear to ear. Even though he knew that day happened when he was almost 30 years younger, it felt like it had just ended a few minutes ago.

It was surreal.

He couldn't believe how good it felt to be back in a body that hadn't dealt with years of mishandling. More than that, though, was how good it felt to be carefree again. As much as he tried to avoid it, the weight of adult responsibility was crushing. It felt like the burden was lighter back when his friends were around. They meant so much to him.

And that first kiss. How did he forget that happened?

He couldn't help but wonder what might have been had Melissa not moved a few towns away at the end of the summer. He remembered how they hung out almost every day up until that point. They kissed a few more times. *When did that stop?* he thought to himself. He already wanted to go back and had to fight the urge to open the book again.

He looked around the library. Every one of those thousands of books contained more than just his memories, but his entire life. He could spend an eternity just going from one good day to the next and living all his best memories over and over again. How could anyone ever tire of that?

He was pulled from that thought by the sound of Matthew clearing his throat. "Ah, I see you are back. So, was that day as good as you remembered?"

"It was somehow even better! My friends were pretty awesome, and as a bonus, I'm not dealing with that sunburn this time around," David laughed. Reliving that day also brought back the memory of slathering himself with aloe for the next week. Even if he did have to endure that sting again though, it would've been worth it.

The old man returned his smile. "There's a reason that book's cover was all white. It was not your only great day that summer; you had plenty of those. But it was by far the best one. It's one that you've dreamed about often since then. One of the top five days of your entire life."

There were mornings when David woke up and could almost taste the salty sea air. Those dreams always led to great mornings simply from the residual happiness. "Top five?! C'mon, that's gotta be like top three. So, is there a limit to how many times I can go back to that one? If I wanted just to keep doing the same day over and over, could I?" he asked half-jokingly.

Matthew laughed. "No, there is no limit, and if you desired, you could relive that same day repeatedly. However, you have more good memories than I think you realize. You don't need to focus on just one great day when so many others are begging to be relived."

A thought had been nagging at the back of his mind since returning from that perfect day. "There's something I don't get about all this...there were details from that day I know I didn't remember. But I remember them now. Before opening that book, I couldn't tell you what I had for lunch or what I wore. Now those memories are as fresh as the ones from yesterday at work. If these books are all written from my memories, how is that even possible?"

"Ah yes, that is because these books are so much more than just your memories, David. They are complete stories of the entire day from your point of view. No detail is missed. When you open one, you are reliving that day the exact same way you did the first time. When you look around a room, you aren't just seeing the things you remember; you are seeing everything as it was. I am usually quite humble, but I must admit that I take pride in my attention to spotting every little detail," Matthew said with a wink.

The amazing opportunity he now had was beginning to dawn on him. He looked over at the rows upon rows of bookshelves, a collection of thousands and thousands of days of his life. There were so many events he would love to do again: concerts, vacations, and that time he hit a game-winning shot in his youth basketball league. Then he thought about all the people he had known who had passed away. He could go back to his childhood and one of the days he spent fishing with his grandfather.

However, the disorienting feeling of coming back from spending time in his teenage body made him wonder what it would be like to go that far back. He decided he was in no rush to find out.

As he went to give the book back to Matthew, he noticed the gold strip just above the numbers was longer than before. He remembered quickly glancing at it before opening it, and although it was there, it was only about the width of a couple of the numbers.

Now, it stretched the whole length of the binding, just like the previous one.

Matthew saw the question coming. "You are wondering about the memory strip. As the name implies, that is a visual representation of how much of a particular day you remember. It's rather helpful. Walking the aisles here lets you easily see which days, good or bad, were memorable. It also shows, in a broader sense, how much of our days we just forget not long after they happen. However, that is more just an aspect of the human condition than any personal flaw."

"Is that why the strip on the days I've gone back to are so long?" David asked.

"Precisely. The events of those days are now fresh in your mind as if you have just lived them for the first time. It's also why those shiny strips tend to be longer on your most recent days," he responded.

"And why none of the first few hundred books have any strip at all…," David added.

"Correct. Time doesn't erase all memories but it plays a factor in dulling them so only the brightest, most impactful ones remain," Matthew explained.

"So, if I'm going to relive more of my past while I'm here…wherever 'here' is…I should stick to the lightly colored books with the smallest strips of gold?" he asked.

"Yes, that is a pretty smart plan. And you have so many good days to choose from. Some were because of places you visited, some because of events like concerts or carnivals or vacations…but the majority of your best ones were because of the people you shared your time with. And that is the key to it all. Most people don't realize, really truly realize, that their days are numbered. If you're lucky, you end up with around 30,000. Most people wind up having far less. There is nothing so precious as time, and when you choose to share it with others, you are sharing the most valuable resource on the planet. Giving time to someone is the same as giving them a little piece of your life." There was something about Matthew's point that struck David hard. He had pretty much cut everyone out of his life.

"I don't know why I stopped sharing my time with my friends. Or my mom. Or anyone else…" He trailed off at that thought. There had to be a reason.

Matthew sighed. "Choices always have consequences and your choices veered away from those that cared about you. But the thing with choices is that, as long as you are living, you can make new ones. But for now, why don't you focus more on the choices you have right here."

David knew that Matthew was right. About all of it, but mostly about the choices he had right now; he could go back and see any part of his life and experience it all just like it was the first time. The only hard part was going to be choosing which day he wanted to go back and do it again.

There was one aspect that he knew, no matter what had to be part of any day he went back to. Even though he knew it wouldn't change his present, he wanted to see his friends again.

"Do I have to wait to go back? Like, am I going to wake up soon, and if I am, can I make sure that I have this dream again tomorrow?" David asked.

"To answer your question, as best that I can, you do not need to wait to visit another day. There are no cool-down requirements here. And you have time to visit another day," Matthew responded, trying his best to mask his unease at the question.

"Ok, perfect." David already had a good idea of the time frame he wanted to visit, just not the exact day. "I think I'd like another day with my friends. Is there a good one with that cute girl I was dating, Vanessa?"

Oof. I was hoping the joy and happiness from that great beach experience as a teenager would distract him and give me more time to figure out what I should do here. The path he wants to follow will not lead him to anything good.

"I thought you might want to visit Drew, Jimmy, and Melissa again. What about a day from your early days in college? I think you might enjoy a day before the stresses of work and bills and all the baggage that came with adulthood," Matthew asked. He tried to sound calm like Vanessa was only a minor player in David's life.

"When did I meet her anyway? It feels weird that I can't remember much about her. Why is that?" David wondered out loud.

"Sometimes we meet people, and they have a momentary impact on our lives, and then they leave. Memories can be selective sometimes when it comes to the people we retain." God, please forgive me for the lies. I can't let him feel that hurt again. But I know I can't completely shut him out, either. I think I know a safe compromise...

Matthew continued, "You met her in college at the end of a pretty great day. Would you like to go back and see her?"

David thought about his time in college. The parts he remembered were all great. He took many classes and always prioritized them but still maintained a fun social life. Melissa went to school a few hours away, but Jim and Drew were there, and together they created some great memories. Weekends were filled with concerts or long hikes or just lounging at the beach. He couldn't remember having any "bad days" during his entire time in college (although there were many stressful periods when finals came around or when grades were posted). He was all for revisiting that era of his life. And getting to see how he met Vanessa would be a bonus.

"That sounds like a damn good idea. Just maybe not any of the days with exams. I could go the rest of my life without having that kind of stress again." David chuckled a little as he said that. Just because he did well in his classes didn't mean he enjoyed them all.

"We can skip those. Junior year, the day after your last final. I'm not sure exactly how much of it you'll recall, but it was one that you thoroughly enjoyed," Matthew said matter-of-factly. He got up to go retrieve it while David sat there, taking in the situation.

At that moment, David realized he hadn't had any time to just think by himself since he first got to this strange place. His time had been spent either walking around confused or talking to Matthew or off reliving his past. He wondered exactly how long he had been having this dream or whatever it was. It had to be more than just one night's sleep, right? He tried to recall his last moment awake, but it was a blurry mix of work, driving, and sitting around his apartment. Did he finally get so caught up in his thoughts that he forgot about the real world and only remembered his dreams?

That would be one hell of a trip, he thought. *Forgetting the real world the way most people forget what they do in their dreams.*

He decided that it wasn't important. At least not right now. He had the opportunity not just to see but completely re-experience the best times of his life. He was getting to feel everything from the days when he was happy. He knew that the situation could change at any moment, and he didn't want to say or do anything that might speed it up. There were way too many memories he wanted to explore, so whatever was going on here was fine by him.

His thoughts brought him to what he could remember about the day that the old man was bringing him. Any day after finishing up finals was a good one, but junior year was probably the most rewarding. He nailed his exams, and he knew it. He only had one year of college left. He lived with his best friends. The details of this particular day escaped him, but he knew that it was way better than his current life. After getting to experience the teenage-awesome-beach day fully, his excitement was building for this one.

David watched as Matthew rounded the corner with a very lightly-colored tan book. It was not the same all-white as before, but only by a few shades. No gold memory strip. Matthew took his seat next to him on the couch and, with a smile, passed it to David. "Here you go. This was the first in a long line of really great days that you lived that summer. I won't spoil all the fun, but I can safely say that you will enjoy this one."

"Can't wait!" David said. And he didn't.

David held the book while looking over at Matthew. He gave him a small nod and smiled as he sat back and opened it up.

21
Book 8038

Dave rolled over on the soft bed and his face was splashed with sunlight. He kept his eyes closed and let the growing warmth slowly wake him up. He stretched out, kicking off his covers, and smiled broadly as he remembered he was done with classes for the year. He could hear music coming from the bedroom next to his and knew it had to be Eddy. He was usually the first one up on the mornings when he was actually here and not at some random girl's place, and he made sure everyone else in the apartment knew it. Dave thought Eddy could be a bit of an egotistical asshole at times, but his boisterous personality came in clutch on multiple occasions. He had lost count of the number of concerts, football games, and wild parties they could get into just through Eddy's smooth talking.

Dave decided there was no reason to go back to sleep, not today. He lay there on his back, hands behind his head, and smiled. Normally, when Eddy was being this loud, this early, he would be starting his day pissed off at the unwelcome wake-up call. No chance of that right now. He was in an optimistic frame of mind and felt like it was giving him a chance to start his day hours earlier than he otherwise would have.

I'll just sleep in tomorrow, he thought to himself as he got up and made his way to the living room. He felt a little off, like he had done this all before, but the feeling quickly passed.

Dave took his time getting his day started. He grabbed a cold piece of pizza and a beer. *Breakfast of champions*, he thought to himself. He decided earlier this week that today, the day after the stress of his last junior year final, would be a completely chill one. No plans; just see where it takes him. He was up for pretty much anything, whether it be an adventurous hike out in the Everglades or sitting around smoking weed and watching movies all day. As long as he was responsibility-free, he was game.

He surveyed the apartment from the kitchen that opened up to the living room. It was a mess, but then again, they never spent much time there. It was basically a hub for sleeping and eating. Pizza boxes were stacked next to the trash can in the kitchen. Empty beer bottles lined the top of the kitchen cabinets (for the aesthetic, of course). A pile of shoes was thrown next to the door. A large, colorful bong was sitting on the coffee table. Eddy was sitting on the couch with a laptop.

He looked up when Dave came into the room. "Hey, hey, look who it is. Get enough beauty sleep?"

"Yeah, thanks for the wake-up call, dickhead," Dave said sarcastically.

"No problem, man! Up for some kayaking today? Keith said we can use some of his while he's out of town." Keith was one of Eddy's long-time friends. They had interned at the same financial firm the previous summer. Dave had hung out with him a few times, but they never really clicked. Keith was the son of a lawyer and came from money. His parents had bought him a "college house," and they went to parties over there regularly. With Dave's more modest roots, they didn't have much in common. Keith seemed like a decent enough guy, though, and was always down for a good time.

He also had about a dozen kayaks they would sometimes take out for river drinking. Guess that's the first stop today.

"Sure thing, man," Dave replied. They hadn't been out on the water in a few weeks, and he was secretly hoping for an invite soon.

Jimmy was the next one up and came grumbling into the room, looking pissed at the early wake-up. Drew was up not long after. Although they were pre-caffeinated, both agreed to the excursion. They spent the next hour getting ready, packing lunches, taking bong hits, and then counteracting the weed with some strong, black coffee. The group headed out to Jimmy's old Ford Bronco and finally made it to the river after picking up some beer. They were able to launch the kayaks from Keith's large backyard.

It felt like the day was officially starting.

Dave carried his kayak to the muddy edge of the murky, brown water. His childhood fears of being snatched up by an alligator faded as he got older, and now, when he would inevitably see the large, scaly creatures slowly sliding down one of the river banks or passing by while he paddled, the feeling was more of cautious wonder than anything else.

None of them were kayaking experts, but they got slightly better over the last couple of years through trial and error. Mostly error, though. All error, actually. Lessons were learned after their first disastrous excursion together. On that initial journey, they drank heavily while mostly letting the flow of the river guide them downstream for a couple of hours. When they finally decided to turn around and head back, the current was too strong for their drunken, uneven paddling. They laughingly gave up after half an hour of making no progress, looking like a bunch of uncoordinated idiots trying to walk up a down escalator. They ended up paddling to the river's edge, two of them falling in the water after trying to jump to land, and Dave ended up losing his paddle, drifting a few hundred yards before finally running aground. It was a mess.

The only upside was that they got to sit around, soaked and sore, getting shit-faced.

Fortunately, paddling against the pretty-weak current wasn't that bad when you were mostly sober. So for every trip since that poorly planned first one, they made their way upstream for an hour or two, mostly in silence except for the occasional complaints about being tired or asking if they were ever going to turn around and start drinking. Once they decided to change directions, they got to sit back, relax, and float down the river.

Oh, what a life.

The slow current ensured that they had plenty of time to crack open the still-cold beers and talk about whatever. Sometimes, it was about girls, sometimes sports, and on rare occasions, about the meaning of life. But most of the time, it was just about whatever random topic of the day they were interested in. Today was no different. The conversation veered in a thousand different directions but seemed to keep coming back to future plans.

Eddy was the only one that already mapped out his whole post-college life. "I'm going straight to law school and then working for Keith's dad. It's already all set. Fucking cakewalk, dude."

"Law school ain't no cakewalk. You're out of your mind. I dated a girl that went…remember Jen? Man, she burned out after the first year. And she was smart as hell." Drew had liked her a lot and was pretty beat up when she moved back home to Kansas.

"I'm just saying, man. Being a lawyer isn't about how smart you are. It's about doing whatever you can to win," Eddy responded. He wasn't wrong.

"Yeah, well, I'm going to do something where I can still have a life and be able to sleep at night. Not all of us are as loose with our morals as you, E," Drew said.

"And what's that? You going to run a non-profit to save the manatees or something?" Eddy asked.

"Nah, man, your mom doesn't need saving." That response elicited laughter from Dave and Jimmy. "Seriously, all I know for sure is I'm going to graduate next year and then figure shit out."

Dave chimed in. "Same with me, man. As long as I can pay the bills and I'm still in driving distance to the beach, I'll consider that a win. A job is just money. If you can't be happy outside of work, what's the fucking point?"

"Damn right. As long as you make enough to keep your belly full and a roof over your head, the work isn't as important as what you do after," Drew added.

"Man, if you guys aren't careful, you're going to end up renting out rooms in the big ass house I'll be buying with that lawyer money," Eddy laughed.

"Yeah yeah…you can make all the plans you want, doesn't mean it'll all work out that way. Life isn't always just lobbing pitches for you to hit. There's curveballs sometimes, man," Jimmy said.

"You know what's crazy? My beer's empty. Throw me another one, Davy," Drew said. Dave grabbed one from the compartment in the back of his kayak and tossed it to him.

"I hate to tell you guys, but we are running low. We have about six left," Dave told them.

"Well, shit, that should work out perfectly. We only got like a half mile till we're back at Keith's house," Eddy replied.

The friends continued floating down the river, talking and drinking. Paddling was only attempted as they got closer to Keith's place, and even then, it wasn't very coordinated. The combination of the hot Florida sun and a case of cold beer had them struggling to get out of the water. They clumsily pulled the kayaks over to the shed and helped themselves to a late lunch courtesy of whatever they could find in the kitchen. Drew was a pretty talented cook and whipped up some tacos. After they ate, Dave passed out and had a dreamless nap on the couch. Jimmy woke him to tell him they were heading back to the apartment. New plans arose. Tonight was going to be spent going out to some bars.

They got back to the apartment to recharge. A quick shower and small dinner were only interrupted by a call from Mel. Dave hadn't heard from her since they all met up during spring break. She had brought her boyfriend, and, to Dave's dismay, he turned out to be a pretty decent guy. They all had a wild time partying and drinking and getting into late-night trouble. Mel still took up a small residence in his heart, but he could never admit that to anybody. Not even Drew or Jimmy knew, although he was sure that they had their suspicions. His own dating life was nothing to brag about. He had a few flings throughout high school and college but never anything serious. Mel was just different to Dave. They always had a closeness that couldn't be tied down to any single description. They still told each other everything, even when it came to relationships.

"Davy! I've been meaning to call! How did your finals go?" He perked up at the sound of her voice.

"Mel! Pretty sure I did awesome, but grades won't be posted until next week. What about you? Aced them all again?" he asked.

"I better have. But it's the same with me. Nothing is posted until next week. How're the guys doing?" She usually kept up with Jimmy and Drew through Dave. They would talk to her occasionally but far less often than Dave.

"We just got back from kayaking. I think we all have a healthy buzz going so a quick stop to eat something before we go bar hopping. Wish you were here!" 'Healthy buzz' may have been an understatement. The combination of sun and alcohol had him feeling pretty damn drunk.

"Sounds like a typical day for you guys, so we better do the same thing when I'm in town in a couple of weeks," she said.

"Sweet! So you're definitely coming?" he asked.

"Of course! JD is coming too. We're going to stay with my mom for a few weeks. I got to tell you, Davy, I think it's getting serious. He's kinda awesome." Dave was hoping she would be coming alone but wasn't upset. They had a great time when JD came with her before. Plus, he made her happy.

"Nah, he seems pretty cool. I'm happy for you, Mel. Seriously." Oddly enough, he was happy she found someone who seemed to treat her well and make her smile. His feelings for her were complicated, but more than anything, she was a close friend.

"Thanks, Davy! I know you always have my back, so that means a lot. Now, we just have to find you a good girl who gets my seal of approval. Are there any potentials?"

"There was that one girl from my anthropology class, but that kinda flamed out. But who knows? I'm sure the right one is out there." Dave had kind of liked that one but, like most girls he dated, he found a fatal flaw that he couldn't look past. This one turned out to only like country music.

Yee-freaking-haw.

"Well, duh. I think the problem is your wingmen need to step up their game! You know I'd help if I could!" And he knew she absolutely would.

"Haha, thanks, Mel. Who knows, maybe I'll meet someone at the bar tonight. I'm already slightly drunk, so my decision-making skills should be on point," he joked.

"Oh, I'm sure they are! Just be safe, and don't do anything you can't undo in the morning!" she said.

Wise words.

All three of his roommates were now annoyingly knocking on his door, telling him to put some clothes on so they could finally leave. "C'mon, Mel, you know I won't do anything too stupid! Listen, the guys are bugging me to get going, so call me later this week with the details for when y'all are coming!"

"You bet! Talk to you soon, Davy!" she said.

"Bye, Mel!" he responded before finally hanging up.

Dave always felt good after hearing from her. And as much as the woulda-coulda-shoulda scenarios sometimes took hold of his thoughts, he had gotten pretty good at just appreciating their friendship. She was an awesome person to have in his life.

That being said, he was hoping to finally meet someone he might be able to settle down with. Or at least someone that he liked enough to want to be around for more than a few weeks.

The group packed into Eddy's Bronco and headed to the downtown strip of bars and clubs. They had a handful that they would typically bounce between. The first stop tonight was Dave's personal favorite, the Sand Bar. It was nestled down a short alley, a little off the beaten path. Once entering the nondescript brick entrance, you felt like you were walking onto a beachside boardwalk at night. The high, black ceiling was made to look like a clear night sky filled with stars. The bars around the large dance floor were tiki huts, and the entire far wall was a full, high-def screen playing a seemingly endless loop of waves crashing onto a dark beach, moonlight glistening on them as they crested. The music always had great variety but with a heavy rotation of reggae.

This was Dave's bar. And it was packed tonight.

The guys got their first round of drinks, and it didn't take Eddy long to find a group of women to start talking to. The two groups joined up at a high-top table in the corner and went from shots to loud talking to more shots to more talking. Dave could barely make out any of the conversation and spent most of the time smiling and nodding, feeling the alcohol take effect, until he noticed someone at the bar.

She was the most attractive woman he had ever seen. He didn't want to stare but couldn't convince his eyes to stop out of fear they would never be blessed with such beauty again. She caught Dave looking at her and sent a hauntingly beautiful smile right at him. He could feel his cheeks immediately and, uncharacteristically, blush as he returned a shy smile. He turned back to his friends to finish his drink, hoping it would give him a moment to compose himself.

They ordered one more round of shots before the groups went to the dance floor. Dave wasn't joining them, though. He turned and set his sights on the woman at the bar. But when he looked back over, she was gone. *Bummer*, he thought, *she was out of my league anyway*. So he followed his friends and the girls they met onto the dance floor.

The music, along with the heavy-handed bartender, were an intoxicating mix. But together, they gave Dave just the right amount of confidence. Enough to get out there and move but not too much where he would make an ass out of himself. He wasn't a very good dancer but wasn't exactly embarrassing himself, either.

Then he saw her again. The beautiful blonde that he had caught eyes with earlier was dancing with her friends not far from Dave.

He turned back around, suddenly nervous again. He felt a tap on his shoulder, and when he looked over, she was facing him.

"Hi," she said, barely audible over the loud, thumping music.

"Hey!" he yelled as he awkwardly tried to hear her.

"I'm Vanessa". Even over the music, he could hear that her voice matched her looks. It was confident and beautiful...*and damn, I'm drunk*, he thought.

"I'm Dave," he said in a voice that was absolutely too quiet for the situation.

She turned her ear to him. "What?" she yelled.

He realized he needed to be a bit louder, so he yelled back, "My name! It's Dave!"

She gently grabbed his shoulders and pulled herself up to his ear. "You want to grab a drink? I can barely hear over here."

Even with the extra effort, they were too close to the speakers, and in his drunken state, he didn't know what she said. "Why don't we go to the bar? I can't hear you."

Vanessa smiled and rolled her eyes while she grabbed his hand and pulled him off the dance floor. He stumbled his way behind her and thankfully made it to the bar without falling over.

The two of them talked for an hour. She was a year younger, majoring in business. She lived on campus. Although she had grown up in Nebraska, she had been in Florida since middle school.

She was the most beautiful girl Dave had ever met. Her eyes were like deep, blue oceans, and he was drowning in them.

Dave never felt anything but completely comfortable with her the entire time they talked. The nervousness disappeared the moment her voice had first reached his ears. It had been a long time since he met someone who had such an immediate effect on him like this. He realized they had been talking so long that he lost track of the time, hopefully not his ride home.

He looked over to the dance floor to see if his friends were still around, and as soon as he turned back toward Vanessa, she kissed him.

His mind went blank. It felt like time stood still. Although the kiss seemed to last forever, it still felt too short.

"You seem kinda awesome, and I just wanted to get that out of the way. That cool with you?" She smiled. *You are so beautiful*, he thought to himself.

"You are so beautiful," he drunkenly said out loud. His eyes got big as he realized he didn't keep those words to himself. She was laughing, and he was embarrassed.

But then she kissed him again and said, "That was so adorable."

He felt completely relieved. "That was totally meant to stay in my head!"

She laughed. "That's what made it so cute!"

He laughed with her. "I'm not just saying this because I'm drunk. You are pretty amazing."

She gave him that beautiful smile once again. "Woah there, buddy. You keep flattering me like that; it might go to my head."

Her friends came over, and she introduced Dave. They all seemed really nice. She told him she had to go. They exchanged numbers and had one last embrace, and she quickly promised not to wait a week before calling.

Dave didn't need to even think of waiting. He was smitten.

It was late, and Dave found the guys back at the bar. Well, he found Drew and Jimmy. Eddy had left with a girl he had just met.

The guys decided to call it a night and found a cab. Dave annoyed his friends by talking about Vanessa the entire ride home.

They stumbled into the apartment, and Dave fell onto his bed, passing out as soon as his head hit the pillow.

22

David opened his eyes to see Matthew, pencil in hand, book in his lap, focused intently on the words he added to the pages. Shadows from a flickering candle added an extra layer of movement. He seemed to be more lost in his writing every time David returned from revisiting a day. His demeanor during these interludes didn't match how he was when talking to David. He was more serious and intense. The movement of the yellow candlelight seemed to give his wrinkles even more depth, making his face look like it was carrying some heavy, unseen weight.

David watched as Matthew put down his pencil and rubbed his eyes. The look of complete exhaustion was hard to hide. But in an instant, he looked over to David and, once realizing he was back, forced a smile. David wanted to ask if he was okay with his writing stressing him out. He thought better of it. Whatever it was, it wasn't good, and he was still riding his high from that awesome day he just got relive. He made a mental note to ask about it at a better time.

"So, did I choose a good one for you?" Matthew asked. David momentarily forgot what he was thinking as the day's events came rushing back to him.

"Absolutely! I haven't thought about those college days in a long time. We had some serious fun back then. Forgot how much I loved being out on the water kayaking, though it might have been all the drinking with good friends that made it so great," David said.

"Yes, you most certainly did have fun back then. The best choices were not always made but you never lacked when it came to friends to share those experiences with. Such a large part of your happiness was tied to the connections you had with those around you, and most of that group of friends had been around a long time. Your bonds to them were very strong," Matthew said.

David knew he was right. Jimmy, Drew, and Mel had all been there for each other through so many of life's trials and shared so many amazing times together. He had other friends who popped into and out of his life, but those three were his rocks.

"My friends were pretty great. I can't believe we stuck together for so long. I really miss them," David responded, feeling somewhat forlorn at how distant those times had become. The memories had faded, but revisiting those days brought back so many strong feelings. Thinking about what his life was like now brought on an overwhelming sense of loneliness.

David knew he had spent years pushing people away but still couldn't figure out why. He had always loved being around others—until he didn't. As much as he wanted to figure out the answer, there was something else that he had to know first.

"What about Vanessa? I don't know how to describe my memories of her. Empty, maybe? I've seen her twice now while I'm reliving those days, and it's like she's there, and I know her, but when I try to grab a thought about any other time with her, it just falls through my hands like water. It's hard to explain." Reliving that night made him want to go back and see her again. Badly.

Matthew suddenly had a pained look on his face. He tried forcing a smile: "Ah...she did seem pretty special. I wouldn't spend much time worrying about that path, though. There are so many other great memories for you to explore!"

There was definitely more to the story. David thought about it for a minute. She was beautiful, fun, and spontaneous. They obviously dated for a while. Matthew was keeping something from him, and he didn't like it.

"I feel like there's something you're not telling me...like, why can't I remember her?" David asked pointedly.

"Look, David, the way your relationship with her ended was painful. I do not wish to go into that right now, not with more pressing, time-constrained issues in front of us..." Matthew trailed off.

"Wait, what do you mean? That sounds pretty ominous." David let out a small, nervous laugh, but it didn't diffuse the sudden tension. Matthew's demeanor was deadly serious.

I wasn't sure if David was ready to follow the path I was about to present to him, but I could not let his mind continue with that line of questioning. As much as it pains me, he needs to be shown at least one truth about his life, and when choosing between physical pain and emotional pain, I have to go with the former.

"An explanation is in order. There are some books here, even though they contain every day that you have lived that you have never really experienced. What they contain isn't a different path or a new set of exciting experiences. These missed days would undoubtedly cause you much pain, and I do not think that I can continue shielding you from them." Matthew said all of this with a level of care and concern that David was not used to.

"So, you're saying there are days from my past that I've totally blocked out?" David thought about a story he had read years ago that described how some people who experienced great trauma could no longer recall anything about certain aspects of their lives. He had wondered if anything like that had happened to him and if that was why his memories before moving away from his friends seemed so incomplete. How would he even know?

Matthew had a look of such empathetic concern that David knew what he was about to say was highly important. "Unfortunately, I am not speaking about the parts of your past that you've blocked out, David. It's your present that I've been keeping from you."

Boom.

23

It felt like the floor had given way, and David was uncontrollably tumbling into a pit of pure confusion. He couldn't understand what that even meant. Synapses were firing blanks; his mind was racing and frozen at the same time. His present?! He was just at work this morning. Or yesterday morning? Time was hard to keep track of here. But just because his days are boring and monotonous doesn't mean they didn't happen. He tried to stay calm, but the anxiety was breaking through his voice.

"Okay, I think you officially lost me. I have no idea what that's supposed to mean. How are you keeping my present away from me?" he asked.

"I'm sorry, David. However, I believe it best to tell you everything at this point. It's time you gain a complete understanding of what's happening and why you are here." The old man's deep blue eyes showed he was truly concerned. They seemed moments away from tears, reddened and glossy.

"Yes. Please. Even with everything that's been going on here, I was not sure it would be possible to feel any more confused...but here we are. What haven't you been telling me?" David's emotions were all over the place. It felt like just minutes ago, he was riding high from spending a day back in college with his friends. He was frustrated and angry and sad all at once and felt like Matthew's cryptic messages were only making things worse. How could Matthew be keeping something from him, something so serious? How could he not see there was more going on than just an extended, complicated dream?

He felt like an idiot.

"What do you remember about your car ride home from work on the night you stayed late?" Matthew asked.

"I remember..." He had to think for a second. The memory seemed oddly distant. "...I remember finishing up, walking to my car, and seeing some flowers on the edge of the parking lot's pavement...I remember turning on some music for the drive...then the radio stopped working..."

"And after that?" Matthew asked.

"I hit the dashboard to try and fix it...I don't know...I can't really remember all the details. I must have either gone out with my coworkers and got drunk... or I just went home and passed out and woke up here." David knew that didn't make sense, though. Matthew wouldn't be asking such leading questions if the night was uneventful.

"You did end up here that night, but it was the accident that sent you, not a dream," Matthew spoke slowly, thoughtfully choosing his words.

"What accide...oh...ohmyGod..." It came back to David all at once. Staying late at work. Being tired on the drive home. Smacking the dashboard when the radio stopped. And then the truck. The memory hit him hard as he remembered losing control of his car. He could hear the sounds of shattering glass and crunching metal. He needed a minute to process. He buried his head in his hands, realizing that this was way more than just an enlightening dream.

Matthew moved closer to David and put his arm on his shoulder. "I am so sorry, David. I was as shocked as you were when I saw it happen. There was nothing I could do to help but try and make your time here as pleasant as possible."

David had a new, troubling thought. He rubbed his eyes and gathered himself enough to speak. There was no point in waiting any longer to ask. "Matthew, I need to know. Did I die in the crash? Is that why I'm here?"

Matthew spoke calmly. "You came very, very close. And you are not out of the woods yet. But you did not die that night, at least not permanently. You have been in a coma since the crash."

"So, is this what happens when you get close to dying? You go to a library and relive parts of your life?" Even though he didn't consider himself a religious person, David had times in his life where he put a considerable amount of thought into what, if anything, came after this life. He never imagined that a library and a strange old man would be a part of it.

"Not exactly. Typically, when someone's life has come to an end, they are met in a beautiful field by the loved ones who passed into the afterlife before them. Then, after being welcomed warmly, they are led to their own life's 'library' where they get to meet their conscience, and at that point, they can relive as much or as little of their life as they wish. That is what makes your current situation so exceedingly rare and special, David," explained Matthew.

David took this all in and returned with the only logical question he could think of. "If that's true, and I don't wake up from this coma, did I miss out on seeing all my friends and family that already died?"

Matthew responded. "Not at all. Speaking only hypothetically, since you are still technically alive, if you do pass away while here, you will have only changed the order of things. All the people who have been most important in your life, but are no longer living, will always be there when you are ready to see them."

"Ok. So, if I have this all straight, I'm not dead, but I was close enough to dying that I ended up in a place typically reserved for dead people. I've been going back and reliving some great days from my past but haven't been experiencing my present at all. And I've been in a coma this whole time..." David trailed off, thinking about all the days he'd been able to live again. He suddenly had a more important question.

"How long have I been in a coma?" he asked. He tried remembering, but time seemed impossible to discern here. It could have been a few hours. Maybe days. He was trying to make sense of a completely senseless situation.

"I will give you all the information that I know for certain, but it is not going to be pleasant." Matthew took a deep breath. "I'm afraid the accident was over a month ago. 33 days to be exact. You are currently in the ICU. The crash broke your left arm, left leg, and a few ribs, and there was some internal bleeding, but the worst part of your injuries was the damage to your brain. You had a severe concussion and fractured skull."

"Wait, wait, wait, go back a second...I've been here over a month?!" David was in shock. He needed time to process all of this. *Has it really been that long? What about my work? Has anyone even noticed that I've been gone?* So many questions.

David spoke quickly, his mouth trying to keep up with his racing thoughts. "What has been going on out there since I've been gone? How do you even know about everything that's happened since the accident if I've been in a coma?"

Matthew calmly continued, "You had originally asked about the books you have never experienced, the ones from your present. They are from your days in the hospital. I have been chronicling them the entire time you've been here. It is not an easy task. You are asleep most of the day, so I only get bits and pieces."

There's the explanation for why David always saw Matthew writing so intensely when David would return from reliving a day. He should have pieced that information together but was too caught up in past experiences. He was sure there was a lesson in there somewhere about taking time to look at the big picture, but he currently had more important matters to focus on.

"What happens if I open one of those books? Will that make me wake up out there?" David asked.

"No, unfortunately, it is not that easy. Opening one of those books will have the same effect as opening any other here. You will relive that day. There are some differences, though. With these, you are physically limited by your injuries, so you can't move, or open your eyes, or speak, and you only come in and out of 'consciousness' briefly throughout the day. Going to any of these will feel very different and unpleasant, but as always, it is your choice if you choose to see for yourself."

"I think I need to," David said without any hesitation. He didn't want to be kept in the dark anymore. Even if he only got a limited picture of what his life was like right now, he wanted it.

"I want you to be very sure about this, David. Your hearing and touch are the only senses working at all, and even those are fairly muted," Matthew said.

"I am certain. I need to know. No matter how much it sucks, it's my life...but if there are any that are better than the others, I'd want to start there." He now noticed the stack of dark brown books on the ground, slightly hidden in the shadow beside the couch.

"There is not a lot that differentiates these days...," he started to say before seeming to remember something. "But there were a few that may be slightly better than the others. Here. Start with this one, and you can decide if you wish to see anything more."

Matthew grabbed the book numbered 13411. He handed it to David. David noticed the numbering seemed different from the other shelves' books. It wasn't a shiny silver color. More of a darkened, matte gray.

"This is from just a few days after the accident. Your body is still badly broken. You will feel that pain, unfortunately, though the medications you are on do help. But if this is the path you are going to follow, this will be an important first step," Matthew explained.

David sat wondering whether he was about to make a mistake. He just found out that not only was this not all some crazy dream, but that he was in a coma and he had spent the last month getting to know his own conscience. *Do I really need to see what my life in a hospital bed is like?*

He wavered momentarily, but his curiosity got the better of him. He sat back and opened the book.

24
BOOK 13411

beep………..beep….……..beep………...beep…….…...beep……

It was dark. He hurt everywhere. He tried but couldn't open his eyes. All he could hear was the steady beep letting him know he wasn't dead. He just wanted to go to sleep.

So he did.

beep.…….….beep.….…….beep………...beep….….…..beep……

How much time has passed? The pain didn't feel as intense as before. Maybe the nice nurse with the soft hands had given him some more pain meds. He loved her so much. He pictured her as a beautiful angel dressed in all white with a glow emanating from her entire body.

He felt a hand on his, gently squeezing it. He wanted to squeeze back, but nothing would move. He could hear a woman's voice. It sounded muffled like he was underwater and someone was trying to talk to him from just above the surface.

Everything slowly faded away again.

beep............beep............beep............beep............beep......

Must've dozed off. *Hope I didn't miss anything*, he thought. He could hear the same woman's voice but still couldn't make out the words. It sounded like his mother's. *I really should have called her more.* He wanted to talk to her, tell her he was sorry for being such a shitty son. But the harder he fought to open his eyes and wake up, the more he felt like he was trapped as nothing more than a collection of thoughts inside an immobile lump of person.

He wished he did things differently. He wished there was some way to fix himself. He was broken in so many different ways.

He was slipping back away...

25

As David returned to the library, he immediately opened his eyes and sat up on the couch. Being stuck in a body that had lost the ability to move at all, even for a short amount of time, was not a pleasant experience. He put the book down on the table in front of him and wiped the tears from his face. It wasn't just the feeling of being unable to move or see or talk; it was the contrast to the amazing days he had already been able to live again. The emotional roller coaster he was riding took him to places he didn't want to go.

But he felt like he had to go. He was no longer thinking about how to change his mundane, predictable life or about a girlfriend who probably broke his heart. That seemed so trivial now. He was thinking about how he might have already lived his last real day, and if so, he would have died without having any real human connection in years.

And it was all his own choices that brought him to this point alone. Great.

He struggled to find the right words, and his anguished look made his pain clear. Matthew decided to break the mounting silence. "I know that was difficult for a number of reasons. Are you okay, David?"

"I don't even know. I knew it was going to be bad, but I was so helpless, and I could barely even think straight. Was it worse than that the first couple of days after the accident?" he asked.

"Yes, unfortunately. There was nothing for me to record that first day. You technically died briefly during the ambulance ride to the hospital. Thankfully, the EMTs were able to bring you back but it was very touch and go there for a bit. The doctors weren't sure if you would pull through," Matthew said.

The explanation was helpful but did nothing to make David feel any better.

"Am I going to make it now? I mean, is that just what my life is going to be, laid up unconscious in a hospital bed until I finally die?" David wasn't sure if he really wanted to know.

Matthew was honest in his assessment. "At this moment, all I know is you have not died, at least permanently. Your soul fled your broken body to this loosely connected place when you first lost consciousness, probably in response to the immediate shock of the accident combined with the physical trauma. However, nothing in life is permanent. Being in a coma is your current state, but it will, at some point, change. What and when that change will be is still unknown."

It wasn't exactly great news, but David was slightly relieved that it wasn't worse. He had other questions anyway and wanted to shake off the dread that was overtaking him.

"Was that my mom there?" He asked.

"It was," Matthew said.

Of all the bad feelings that were flooding David's mind, the one that was coming on the strongest was guilt about his elderly mother having to travel all that way. Ever since he moved up here, his calls to her had diminished to the point of only reaching out on holidays. And yet, here she was, visiting her middle-aged son in the hospital just a few days after he arrived. Before all this, he always had excuses for why he couldn't go visit. They weren't very good ones. Or the truth.

He just didn't want to go.

"You said that was just a few days after the accident. How long was she there?" David asked finally.

"She got to the hospital on the morning of the day you just visited. She has come back each day since. From what I've been able to hear, your boss, Tom, has put her up in a nearby hotel," Matthew explained.

David was struggling to fight back the tears. "Seriously?! I had no idea he would do something like that for me."

"Tom was not someone you let get close to you, but he still considered you a good person. He came by on the following day and insisted she let him cover the cost." He said.

David could feel himself tearing up again. He did not like being this emotional but couldn't help it. It had been a long day.

Or, more accurately, a long month.

David shook his head. "I need to tell her I'm sorry. She shouldn't have traveled so far just to see me like that. I have been a pretty poor excuse for a son for a long time."

"Your mother was not the only one to come to see you after the accident. Just because you haven't let anyone get close to you doesn't mean people suddenly stopped caring. Distance may have presented you with that illusion. Here, I know that it isn't pleasant, but there is another day from the hospital that you should visit if you are up for it."

Matthew reached down to the stack of books next to him and pulled one from the middle. David may have been mistaken, but it seemed to be a slightly lighter shade of brown than the others—not by much.

"Who else came to see me?" David wondered aloud.

"Many people. Some were unexpected. I mentioned your boss, Tom. He made a couple of visits. A few of your coworkers sent flowers. Even your nice elderly neighbor Martha, the one you've helped with groceries on a number of occasions, sent a nice card. But the day in this particular book was different and I think it best if you experience it without any spoilers." As he explained this, Matthew kept a straight face, not giving any hint at what David might expect.

David wondered who else there might be, but a few names came to mind. He hadn't talked to them in a long time, though.

"Okay. But how will I know? I can't open my eyes or move or anything like that and could barely even hear anything last time," David told him.

Matthew was ready with some helpful information, "This is a couple of weeks after the crash. You will notice that your hearing is a bit improved compared to the day you just returned from, and with the meds lessened, you don't continually fade in and out as much."

"Well, that's a step in the right direction, I guess. Would be nice to see too, but I guess that's not happening anytime soon." David was frustrated about all of this. He just went from thinking that he was having the most amazing, enlightening dream about all the things he missed most in life to finding out he was terribly hurt in a car crash and in a coma with no ability to wake up. Kinda felt like all the 'lessons' he was learning from visiting the past were now rendered pointless.

But none of that diminished his curiosity. Even with the completely foreign feeling of being trapped in a useless body, he had to know.

David sat back again and opened the book.

26
BOOK 13423

beep………..beep..………..beep…………..beep…………..beep……

It took a few minutes for his hearing to fully kick in, almost like an old computer that buzzed and whirred as it slowly booted up. His ears started picking up the sounds around him. First was the machine that beeped along with his heartbeat, although he never really counted that one. It was a sound that ran in the background anytime he wasn't passed out and felt vaguely like an alarm clock, except for the fact he liked hearing this one and had no ability to hit the snooze button. It meant he wasn't dead yet. The sounds expanded out a bit to the noises of people nearby…he assumed it was most likely doctors or nurses checking on him.

It was different today.

Even though they were barely speaking above a whisper, David could make them out almost instantly. Drew and Jim! Holy shit! He wanted to get up so bad. He hadn't seen his best friends in almost a decade. They checked in on each other every year or two, but David always assumed they just did that out of necessity. Except they were here! He could tell they were standing near the edge of his bed, down by his feet.

He heard Jim's deep, raspy voice first. "Man, this sucks. Haven't seen Davey in this kind of shape since he downed half that bottle of tequila and passed out on some lawn chairs. You think they tried slapping him around a little bit?"

Great idea, Jim. Why don't you give that a shot?

"I think that only works when you're shit-faced and find out parents are on the way home early," Drew responded with a small chuckle. David could remember being told about that night. Couldn't really remember it himself, but the story always made him laugh.

"Hey, it worked! He was fucking hammered one minute and bright-eyed and bushy-tailed the next. You had to walk his ass back home," Jim laughed.

Drew was laughing too, "Walking might be overstating it. We were both drunk and stumbled through a bunch of backyards before puking in his garden and passing out."

David remembered waking up the next morning when the sprinkler started spraying them. It was his first hangover, and it was not pleasant. But he wouldn't trade those times for anything.

David wanted to laugh with them.

Another voice now joined his friends. It was a woman.

"Oh, you guys were a mess back then." Another blast from the past. Wait, was that...

"Melly-Mel! I thought you were flying back out today," said Drew.

Melissa came too? Damn. Here he was broken and unable even to open his eyes and see them, but they showed up anyway.

"And miss out on all these good stories? I think not," she laughed. "Besides, Ms. Z asked if I wanted to grab dinner. She wants all the gossip on JD's new wife, and I couldn't say no to having that kind of fun."

David's mom had always loved Melissa. She used to call her the daughter she never had. And David knew that his mom had been spending more time with her since she divorced JD, now that they could bond over their asshole ex-husbands.

"Where is she at? Gotta be careful what we bring up with her around," Drew asked.

"Middle-aged and still scared of getting in trouble? You know, she only pretended not to know about all the shenanigans you guys got into back then," Melissa answered.

The three of them laughed a little more and started talking about some of the other good times they had. David knew he missed his friends, but hearing their voices just made it worse. He wanted to wake up right now, but just wanting it wasn't going to make it happen.

The talk turned to David's current state.

"He's going to pull through. He's a tough fucker. There's no way he goes out like this," Jim said.

"He better pull through. He really needs to move back home. I hate that he's been up here alone for so long. Kinda miss having him around," Melissa responded.

"I don't know. Pretty sure you know the reason he hasn't been back. That night. You remember how he was after it happened. I've never seen anyone just completely broken the way he was. I couldn't even imagine how I would have reacted if I was in his shoes, but he was never the same after," Drew added.

David had trouble following along. What night were they talking about? He just wanted to start fresh somewhere new.

"I wish there was more we could've done to help." Melissa paused. "Did he ever talk about what happened?"

"Not after he moved away. I wasn't going to bring it up either. No need to open up old wounds," said Drew.

David was lost. He could not remember what they were talking about, and it sounded like a big deal. He tried to remember what happened just before he moved away, but those memories had been wiped clean.

"Yeah, I wasn't going to bring it up either. Still hard to wrap my head around it happening. Just so damn random. I know he felt guilty about it, but I have no doubt he did everything he could," Jim said.

"I know he did. I'm sure that's what made it worse. But he is still right here, and he's going to wake up, and we are going to find a way to help him get through this." Melissa sounded like she was holding back tears. He could feel her hand on his as she spoke.

David was slipping back into that quiet darkness. He tried to fight, but it was pointless. He wanted just a little more time to listen to his friends, but their voices grew more distant and muted.

He would have to settle for another dreamless sleep.

27

David was back in his usual spot, lying comfortably on the soft leather couch. Matthew was nearby writing again but put the pencil down when he noticed David had returned. He could immediately tell from the pained look on David's face that he was struggling through some difficult questions.

David was feeling such a mix of unpleasant emotions. He missed his friends so damn much and hated himself for staying away from them. They came so far just to see him laid up, broken, in a hospital bed. They still cared about him. But something they were saying had left him more confused than ever. He hadn't given much thought about what happened just before he moved away from his home and his friends in...well, maybe since he actually left. *What were they talking about? What happened to me that was so bad?* he thought. *I moved away a few years after college to find a good job, not to get away from anything. Right?!*

Something was scratching at the back of his brain, though. Memories buried deep underground were trying to claw their way back up to the light. He strained to remember, but it was useless.

David knew that Matthew would have the answers. "I need to see when it all started. When I pushed everyone away. I need to know why I did that."

I knew this moment would come at some point, but I still wasn't ready even with years to think about it. There was a reason David couldn't remember. I wanted to protect him. But with everything else that had happened, I knew it was time for the truth. David deserved to have that gap in his memory filled. He needed the chance to deal with the pain.

"David, that is a memory you had locked away a long time ago. It was a painful one to live through, and you swore never to think about it again. I did my best to honor that wish," Matthew explained.

"I don't care what I said before! I need to remember!" David tried not to raise his voice, but he had to know why he had abandoned his friends and what was so bad that he couldn't even go back and visit them.

Matthew knew that there was no use in delaying it further. No more subterfuge. Once David set his mind to something, there wasn't any way to talk him out of it. That was a part of his personality that never changed. "If that is what you want, then I will help you. But please know, this will bring you great pain."

"I understand, but I can't be in the dark anymore," David responded.

Matthew got up from his spot on the couch and motioned David to follow him. They made their way past rows and rows of David's memories until getting to a set of bookcases Matthew hoped he would never have to see again. The shelves looked like any of the others in the library with one small exception, hardly noticeable to David until now. The vertical slats here were doubled up. Matthew put his hands on them and slowly pushed them aside, revealing hundreds more books. The majority of them were very lightly colored, some even bright white signifying the best of David's days. None of them had even the faintest glimmer of the gold memory strips. Matthew pointed to the one that he was looking for. 10219. It was completely black, as was much of the next couple of shelves following it. They seemed hidden beneath unnatural shadows.

David was confused. "I thought you said I could relive any day I wanted? It looks like at least a year or two of memories that you had hidden from me."

"I'm sorry, David. This was a part of your life that you wanted to forget, and I did what I felt I had to do. It was not something I took lightly. I struggled with the decision. Part of me wanted nothing more than to shield you from any pain. I hid these memories away as best as I could. Even so, you still had small flashes from time to time," he said.

"I need to know what happened. I need to know why I am the way I am now," David explained.

"I understand that. And it wasn't long after hiding these memories away that I realized it was a mistake, but not one I thought could be made better by simply making you suddenly remember. As painful as reliving that day will be for you, I hope it at least sheds some light as to why you wanted to be protected from all of this and how it was so easy for me to help in any way I could," Matthew said as he motioned to the cases.

David slowly reached for the book and pulled it off the shelf. It might have been a figment of his imagination, but the book felt heavier than the others. He looked over to Matthew, who gave him a small nod, his eyes welling up with tears. Matthew turned to walk back toward the couch, and David followed.

As they walked, both were silent. David could not stop thinking that there was something so terrible in his life that he gave up everything he ever knew and loved just to get away from it. Matthew's thoughts, however, were on how best to show David that that night did not define him as much as his response to it did.

David took a seat without saying a word. They both knew that the contents of the book in his hands already had a profound impact on his life and wondered what the impact of living it again would be.

"Reliving that day will unlock many memories attached to it. I know that you do not yet understand the effect that that day had on your life, but there were so many others that will now be re-added to your life story. Please understand that no matter what you experience on this day, it does not change who you are or who you can still be." Matthew wished he could live the day with David, to help him through it, and see that he made it to the next one in better shape. But he knew that he was helpless in that regard. He was limited to the same bystander role he had the first time.

Unlike any of the previous books David experienced, there was a touch of fear in what he would find within these pages. "Could you give me a little warning about what's in this? I know it's bad, but was the whole day bad, or is there just some sort of short, terrible event?"

"There is no warning or advice I could give to help you get through this part. I should not have kept this from you for so long..." Matthew hesitated, choosing his words carefully. "I can tell you that the day did not start as if it would be such a negative turning point in your life."

"I guess I'll just dive in then…" David responded while sitting back.

Matthew placed his hand on David's shoulder. "And I will be here waiting for your return."

28
BOOK 10219

David was gently awakened by the sound of music. He had recently begun picking out different songs to set as his alarm and believed they helped set the tone for his day. On the mornings that he planned to work out, he would pick some high-tempo, upbeat songs. If he had an important project at work, he would go with a classic 80's montage track, like "Eye of the Tiger" or "The Final Countdown." But today was different. He started the day with the almost annoyingly happy melody from "Mr. Blue Sky" by Electric Light Orchestra.

He waited until the chorus started before turning it off. He didn't care if it was cheesy. The song always brightened his mood. Not that today needed the extra push. When he looked over at the clock on his nightstand, there was a folded piece of paper on top of it. He opened it up and read:

Good morning, sleepyhead!

I almost woke you up to 'workout' ;) with me, but you looked too peaceful. I cut up some melon in the fridge (even though I know you'll just be having Pop-Tarts for breakfast). Hope you have an amazing morning! Can't wait for dinner tonight!

Love always,

Nessa

With a beaming smile stretched across his face, David eagerly got out of bed. He went over to the top drawer of his dresser and peeked under his rolled-up socks. That's where he kept the ring he finally paid off last week. *Today's the day*, he thought to himself. *I can't believe I'm finally going to do it.* He had been planning this for months, and just as he had expected, the butterflies in his stomach were already swarming. He grabbed his phone and started checking in with his friends.

He had some errands to run before meeting up with everyone for lunch. There was some wine to buy. Maybe some champagne. He had to pack a bag for the beach tonight. That's where he planned to get down on one knee, the same beach they had gone to so many times together. He figured he could knock all this out pretty quickly, so he took the extra time during the morning to just relax. Or try to.

But he was a ball of nervous energy.

He started cleaning every inch of the apartment, folding clothes, and dusting—things he never did without some external force pushing him to do them. He just wanted to stay busy and keep his mind occupied, but his thoughts kept returning to the fact that, hopefully, by tonight, Vanessa, the most amazing person he had ever met, would be his fiancé.

Time felt like it was moving in slow motion. Finally, he got a text from Drew that they were on their way and that, in Drew's words, *he better have his ass ready for some day drinking.*

Not that he needed much prodding today.

David got to the restaurant and saw his friends, already with drinks in hand, sitting around a large corner table. Even with the craziness of their lives, they still got together at least once every week or two. As he walked toward them, they looked up and let out a loud chorus: "DAVY!"

"Hey guys! Where's my drink?" David responded.

"You know we got you, man! Rum and coke are already on its way," Jimmy told him.

David smiled and took a seat next to Jimmy. They already knew his plans to ask Vanessa to marry him that night. He figured it would be great to see his friends first, which would hopefully help calm his nerves a bit.

"Don't have too many, though. You don't want to pass out when you go down on one knee," Melissa said.

Jimmy laughed. "That would be pretty damn memorable, though. Especially if she had to call us to come pick your ass up."

"Yeah, yeah, that's not going to happen. I'm not getting too drunk until after she rejects me," David said with a smile.

"You know damn well she's going to have a very emphatic 'yes.' You guys are nauseatingly good together," Drew said.

"All I know is you better call me as soon as it's official," said Mel. He was the first one that she called after JD proposed to her.

"You know I will! I still can't believe I'm finally doing this!" David said.

"Hey, never too late to back out. You can join me in my lifelong quest of no-strings-attached dating," said Jimmy. He loved the single life and made it a point never to let a relationship go past 3 months. No matter how much we tried selling him on really getting to know someone and caring about them, he wasn't buying it.

"Oh please, you know you're the only one who could live that life. The rest of us actually appreciate the ups and downs that you only get when you love somebody," Melissa told him.

"The downs can suck, but as long they don't last long, it's still worth it," JD chimed in. David sensed something behind the comment and the way he glanced at Melissa.

"See, with me, I don't have to worry about any downs. No feelings hurt, no drama, no being worried I might say the wrong thing and piss her off. I just get to be myself and move on when we both feel like finding something new. It's really a win for everybody involved." As much as Jimmy tried to rationalize it, David knew he was missing out.

"I don't know, man. You may not have any 'downs,' but you don't get the 'ups' either. I think you're going to find some awesome girl that likes the same things you do and that you like being around, and you won't even realize you're falling for her until she goes to leave one day, and you don't want her to. It's going to happen," David explained; all the while, Jimmy was shaking his head.

"Nope, nope, nope. Telling you, not going to happen. I can't be tamed, man! I'm like a wild buffalo. I gotta roam." Melissa rolled her eyes as Jimmy spoke.

"I mean, you smell like a wild buffalo," Drew retorted.

The group laughed, had another round of drinks, and eventually ordered lunch. They had their typical great time to

As they had one last drink before parting ways, the conversation turned to David's plans for tonight. They knew he was planning to do it on the beach, but he had been vague about the details. That was mostly because he didn't quite know the details either, but he spent the night before planning out the specifics.

"So, we are going to that spot just past the boardwalk, and I'm laying out a blanket. I've got some wine, and I'm going to turn on some music, and then I'm going to talk to her about how much I love her and then get down on one knee and pull out the ring," came the long-winded explanation.

"Just don't talk too long unless you're bringing her some coffee," Jimmy said with a laugh.

"Shut up, Jimmy! I think that sounds very romantic, Davy," Melissa told him.

"Thanks. We'll see how much of it I can do before my nerves get to me," David told her.

David felt oddly out of place. A mix of dread and deja vu seemed to wash over him. The feeling passed quickly, and he didn't give it a second thought.

They all said their goodbyes. David promised to text the group as soon as he proposed. He still had a few hours before Vanessa got off work, so he went back to the apartment and called his mom.

She spoke first. "Oh, Davy, I'm so happy this is finally happening. Now, when are you going to give me those grandkids I've always wanted?"

"Mom! One thing at a time!" David laughed.

"I know, I know. I'm just so excited. I get to have a daughter! You know, besides Melissa." David's mom had always considered his tight-knit group of friends her extended family. Years ago, they even started calling her "mom."

"I'm definitely nervous, but I'm going to try to take a short nap before we meet up for dinner," David explained.

"Are you going to ask her at dinner?" his mom asked.

"I thought about it, but I decided I wanted it to be more private. It's supposed to be perfect weather tonight, so I'm taking her to the beach after dinner, and I'm doing it there," David told her.

"Oh, that sounds lovely! She is going to be so happy, and I'm so happy for both of you." David could tell his mom was feeling emotional as her voice cracked just a little.

"Thanks, Mom. Look, I've got to go so I can try to calm my nerves a bit. But I love you, and I'll call you first thing tomorrow morning with an update," David said.

"Oh, you better! and I love you too, David," she said before they hung up.

David, still slightly buzzed from the lunch drinks, set an alarm and laid down on his couch. He drifted off into a deep but dreamless sleep. He woke up to the sound of an annoyingly loud ringing, feeling slightly less tipsy but now with a sudden need for some really strong black coffee. He still couldn't help smiling, remembering that his soon-to-be fiancé would be getting over there shortly. Wanting to shake off some of the lingering cloudiness (possibly a blend of day drinking and a great nap), he took a steaming hot shower while the coffee was brewing.

He could hear Vanessa's keys unlocking the door as he was walking into the kitchen in his towel.

"Oh hey, handsome. Please tell me that's your outfit for dinner," she smiled as she came closer for a hug.

"Only if you wear a matching one," David pulled her closer and kissed her. Even after the last few years and the thousands of kisses, each one felt like the first time their lips touched in that bar.

"You know, I totally would, but I already wore all my nice towels this week and can't be seen wearing an old one in public," she said jokingly.

"Valid excuse. Hey, let me just get dressed, and then we could head out. Kinda want a drink or two before dinner," he said.

"No arguments here! I think I'm feeling margarita-ish," she replied.

They got to the bar, still laughing and smiling at each other. It was one of those nights where it felt like no one else existed. As Drew so eloquently put it, they were nauseatingly good together.

Dinner was perfect. They went to the same restaurant where they had their first real date. They laughed about their first kiss at the bar. They talked about the future they both wanted, buying a house, starting a family, and going on vacations to faraway places.

Every now and then, throughout the dinner, David would look up at Vanessa and say to himself:

"I am the luckiest guy in the world."

And he truly believed it. Not only was she the most beautiful woman that David had ever met, but she was smart and funny and loved his friends and liked the same movies, and had the same taste in music. In the years they were together, they never once had an awkward silence or big fight or disagreement about what they wanted in the future.

She was perfect for him, and he thanked God that they found each other.

After dinner, David and Vanessa headed to the beach. They parked at their usual spot at the small boardwalk that went over the dune. David's nerves were already firing off in every direction.

Besides the wind picking up a little, the weather was perfect, with only a few clouds passing briefly in front of the bright, full moon. It gave the sand a beautiful, ghostly glow. The sound of the loud waves crashing was only accompanied by the gentle water rushing up the shoreline. Besides that, silence. That was always

David's favorite thing about coming to the beach at night: Nothing but the stars and waves.

They made their way to a nice spot not far from the boardwalk and laid out the blanket. The picture David had in his mind of lying and talking to Vanessa about how much he loved her before pulling the ring out of his pocket wasn't going to happen. His nerves were too much, and he knew if he didn't just do it now, he'd chicken out. So, as her back was turned while she was bent over reaching in the backpack for the bottle of wine, he got down on one knee and clumsily dug in his pocket for the box.

When she turned around and saw him, she dropped the bottle into the sand as her hands covered her mouth.

"Oh my God, is this for real?" she asked through her fingers.

David reached for her hand and asked her, tremblingly, "Vanessa, will you marry me?"

He placed the ring on her finger. "Yes!" she said.

"Yes!" she yelled.

They embraced and kissed, and David felt at peace. After knowing for so long that he wanted to spend the rest of his life with Vanessa, the most beautiful, perfect woman he had ever met, he finally got up the nerve to ask her. And she said yes. The butterflies were gone, replaced with a warm feeling of pure happiness. He was officially going to marry the girl

"I'm really glad you said yes because otherwise, the champagne would have felt a little wasted," David said as he pulled the bottle from his bag.

"Well, I'm looking forward to both of us feeling a little wasted after this. I can't believe we are getting married!" she said.

"Come on, you didn't have any idea that I was asking you tonight?" David asked.

She laughed. "I thought you might sometime soon, and once we got here tonight, I started to wonder...but you still find ways to surprise me."

They laid back and talked and laughed and finished the bottle of champagne, then opened the bottle of wine, and shortly after were sufficiently drunk. Their heads were swimming in the pleasant euphoria that only comes in situations like these, situations where two people, completely in love with each other, can find perfect moments together. And David felt that this night on the beach was perfect. They were both totally content with staying here all night, laughing, talking about their future life together, and singing (poorly) along with whatever music was playing on their little radio.

Suddenly, Vanessa stood up. "Davy! Let's go swimming!"

"I'll try," David said. As he attempted to stand up, he realized it was a bad idea. He fell back onto the blanket, laughing. Vanessa laughed, too.

"Well, I'm going. You can watch!" Vanessa said. She stood up, tipped slightly to her left, then regained her balance by holding her hands to her sides. "See, I'm good!"

"Sure you are!" David laughed.

Vanessa pulled off her shirt, and then slid her jeans off too, throwing them at David. "Your loss!" And she blew him a kiss as she turned toward the shadowy dark water and ran to it.

David watched her jump over the first wave and smiled as he laid back down and stared into the black velvety sky. The darkness came in waves, first from the clouds passing before the moon, then from his eyes closing.

He wasn't sure how long he was out when he thought he heard a yell coming from the water. It was short and barely audible over the loud crashing waves. He reached over on the blanket and realized

Vanessa wasn't back yet. His alcohol-fueled thoughts were slogging toward reality. He stood up, stumbled a bit, then regained his balance while trying to look out toward the darkness of the rumbling ocean.

He couldn't see anything except the sea foam on the crashing waves. He started walking toward the oncoming water.

"Vanessa!" he yelled to the void before him.

No response. He began looking up and down the coastline. *Maybe she swam out a bit, and the current pulled her down the shore*, he thought.

He started walking down the coastline, calling out her name. A pit in his stomach grew.

"VANESSA!" His yells were getting more desperate. *Where is she?*

He wandered back to where she first got in the water, his voice growing frantic as he kept calling for her.

No response.

He waded into the water and was only knee-deep when he felt the tremendous pull of the ocean. He recognized it immediately: A strong, dangerous rip current. He ran back to the blanket and grabbed his phone to call for help.

He called 911 and went back down to the water. He tried going out until the water was at his waist, but it was pointless. The moon had disappeared behind some clouds creating darkness so thick that David couldn't see more than a few feet in front of him. But he had to keep looking. She was out here somewhere, and he wasn't going to stop until he found her.

He wasn't sure how long he was in the water when the first flashing lights made their way onto the dune. As soon as he saw them, he ran from the darkness, hoping they would be able to help.

Everything was a blur.

He told the first officers about how they had just gotten engaged and then started drinking and how she decided to go for a night swim but that he was too drunk to follow. About how he didn't know how long she was in the water before he realized she was gone. More police and paramedics showed up. Some went out to the water with flashlights. The officer he was talking to told him they had boats on the way.

There were questions. So many questions. David tried to answer as best he could, but his head was clouded with alcohol and despair. How much did she drink? What was she wearing? Was there any arguing before she ran off? How long were you looking for her before you called 911? Was she a good swimmer?

Is there any family we should contact?

Paramedics came over to him. They insisted on checking him out. He insisted he was fine; he just had to keep looking for Vanessa.

He could see a boat coming across the horizon, bright beams of light pointing towards the dark water. A few hundred yards from the shoreline, it slowed down. Now, it was crawling forward, slowly swinging its lighted eyes from side to side.

Then the light stopped swinging.

David watched as the vessel moved closer to the light's point. Even from his vantage point on shore, through the blackness of the night, he could see the officers lifting something out of the water.

He waited for what felt like an eternity. Finally, he overheard the word that broke him on one of the nearby officer's walkies.

"Deceased."

David fell to the ground, losing consciousness on the way.

29

There was no proper way to prepare David for the day he just chose to experience again. Vanessa was the love of his life, and even though I hid away the bulk of his memories of her, they would all be coming back now. When I first set this all up, I couldn't completely erase her from his past. She was such an integral part of his life. I left most of their first couple years together untouched and carefully chose the day after one of their few fights as the first day that would be hidden. Hiding away painful memories is not forbidden, but I must admit that I took it a step further and definitely broke some rules. For that, I am sure I will have to pay a price, but you must know that I was only trying to protect David.

As I waited by that previously hidden set of bookcases, the small memory strips began to shine. When he returned, he would know exactly what he had lost. It would not be pleasant, but I think he needs to relive it one more day. He must be shown how much his friends cared for him.

He needs to know that he was always worthy of love and that we can not define ourselves by the worst things that happen to us.

It may be the last bit of wisdom I can share.

I was now in a mad scramble to find out what was happening in the real world too. I knew that the doctors working on David were losing hope about him ever waking up. There was talk that his brain injuries might be too severe ever to come back from.

I knew that my time teaching David lessons would either end soon or be extended indefinitely with his death. As much as I loved the unique opportunity I was given, David deserved a chance to improve his life before it ended.

Or, he should at least get to make that choice himself.

I began planning a last-ditch effort to help give him that option. I believe it's typically called a Hail Mary play. I would have to break a couple more rules, but if it worked, David might have a chance to live the rest of his life. And if he learned any lessons while here, he might get to live those years happily. Whatever punishment I might face would be worth it if I got to make things right with David.

30

David awoke back on the same spot on the couch. Matthew was sitting next to him. He felt a terrible blend of guilt and sadness. Tears were streaming down his cheeks. The pain felt fresh. The book dropped to the floor as he sat up and buried his face in his hands. *How could he have been so weak? Why didn't he do more?*

She was supposed to be his wife. Their future together is what gave him meaning and purpose. All of the feelings he had repressed for the last decade came flooding back. Her last words seemed to taunt him.

Your loss.

He wanted to scream to her, *"You don't even know. Losing you made me lose myself."* Vanessa was David's world while they were together, but once she was gone, his life meandered aimlessly, like a rudderless ship at sea. The only direction he had was one away from hurting.

It had all made sense now why he moved away. Why he never went back. Why, after the beach had long been his sanctuary, he now avoided going anywhere near it.

And David could not stop thinking about Vanessa now. The memories roared back the way smoldering embers doused with gasoline would explode in a fiery blaze. He had loved her so much, and yet he had never even thought of her in all the years since it happened. That realization made David hate himself even more.

He could have saved her.

There was a hopelessness that had overtaken him. The woman he loved, that he had just proposed to, died, and he didn't do anything but run away. How could anyone still care about someone like that?

But now, the thought of his friends coming to see him in the hospital made him feel different. For some reason, they never gave up on him.

He thought a lot about how his own choices shaped his pain and how he has always had the ability to turn it all around. He had to choose to let people back in and find a way to forgive himself.

He had to let go of his hurt.

He looked up at the old man sitting next to him. His eyes were swollen with held-in tears. It dawned on David that Matthew had lived through it all, too. He had chronicled his entire relationship with Vanessa and had to know more than anyone else how much she meant to him.

David finally spoke. "I understand why you kept the memories of that night from me. But it hurts even more knowing she has not had any place in my thoughts for so long."

"David, I know that you are still in pain over what happened. There have been mornings, many of them, where I knew you had seen her in your dreams. She was special to you...perfect...but not even that word does your relationship justice. You lost someone you loved a great deal, most tragically. You lost part of yourself that night. The part that cared deeply, that loved life and everything in it.

30

David awoke back on the same spot on the couch. Matthew was sitting next to him. He felt a terrible blend of guilt and sadness. Tears were streaming down his cheeks. The pain felt fresh. The book dropped to the floor as he sat up and buried his face in his hands. *How could he have been so weak? Why didn't he do more?*

She was supposed to be his wife. Their future together is what gave him meaning and purpose. All of the feelings he had repressed for the last decade came flooding back. Her last words seemed to taunt him.

Your loss.

He wanted to scream to her, "*You don't even know. Losing you made me lose myself.*" Vanessa was David's world while they were together, but once she was gone, his life meandered aimlessly, like a rudderless ship at sea. The only direction he had was one away from hurting.

It had all made sense now why he moved away. Why he never went back. Why, after the beach had long been his sanctuary, he now avoided going anywhere near it.

And David could not stop thinking about Vanessa now. The memories roared back the way smoldering embers doused with gasoline would explode in a fiery blaze. He had loved her so much, and yet he had never even thought of her in all the years since it happened. That realization made David hate himself even more.

He could have saved her.

There was a hopelessness that had overtaken him. The woman he loved, that he had just proposed to, died, and he didn't do anything but run away. How could anyone still care about someone like that?

But now, the thought of his friends coming to see him in the hospital made him feel different. For some reason, they never gave up on him.

He thought a lot about how his own choices shaped his pain and how he has always had the ability to turn it all around. He had to choose to let people back in and find a way to forgive himself.

He had to let go of his hurt.

He looked up at the old man sitting next to him. His eyes were swollen with held-in tears. It dawned on David that Matthew had lived through it all, too. He had chronicled his entire relationship with Vanessa and had to know more than anyone else how much she meant to him.

David finally spoke. "I understand why you kept the memories of that night from me. But it hurts even more knowing she has not had any place in my thoughts for so long."

"David, I know that you are still in pain over what happened. There have been mornings, many of them, where I knew you had seen her in your dreams. She was special to you…perfect…but not even that word does your relationship justice. You lost someone you loved a great deal, most tragically. You lost part of yourself that night. The part that cared deeply, that loved life and everything in it.

I think you realize that now. But you didn't lose the love of those closest to you. Your mom. Drew. Jim. Melissa. I think you should go back and see one more day, a few days after the accident. It will be painful. There is no getting around that. However, you need to see the choices you made that day."

David didn't want to go there. He knew what he would face. The feelings he was going to have to feel all over again. But part of him felt like he owed it to Vanessa. He pushed any thought of her so far back in his mind for so long that she was all but forgotten. He needed to remember her. He needed to feel that loss and find a way to deal with it.

"Ok. I'll do it," David told him, feeling like this was his penance.

"I know that there is nothing you will remember from what I'm going to say now while you are there, but it needs to be said anyway. You had reached your lowest point that day. But you survived. You did not give up on life. That is the most important choice you have ever made," Matthew explained somberly.

David lowered his head, unsure if that was the right choice. But he knew he had to go back and see and feel it all again.

For Vanessa.

Matthew already had the book on the table in front of them. 10223. Unsurprisingly, all black.

"This is a few days after that terrible night," Matthew explained as he passed it to David.

Without another word, he sat back, fresh tears still running down his cheeks, and opened the book on what would undoubtedly be another painful experience.

31
BOOK 10223

David's head was pounding. He rolled over and fell off the couch he had passed out on the night before. He recognized the room but couldn't immediately figure out why he was in Drew's house. The fresh smell of alcohol alerted him that he had knocked over a bottle. He glanced at it, and instead of picking it up, he got up and quickly rushed to the bathroom.

He threw up a few times but somehow felt even worse when he looked in the mirror. He didn't recognize the reflection. His eyes were bloodshot with bags underneath. A patchy, scraggly beard had taken residence on his face. His hair was unkempt and appeared not to have been washed in days. His white t-shirt had some unknown stains and an unpleasant odor emanating from it.

He was a mess.

When he returned to the couch, he picked up the spilled bottle and finished what was left. He was operating on some type of self-destructing autopilot.

He saw a note left for him on the coffee table:

Don't forget to get cleaned up today. Picking you up at 2. Call if you need anything at all. Jimmy will be there sometime in the morning.

    -Drew

David looked at the clock and saw it was only 9. He told himself that if he got up and shaved now, he could go back to sleep for a bit.

Laying back down on the couch, he finally started piecing together why he had to get cleaned up and why Drew was picking him up later.

Vanessa's funeral.

He was going to be sick again.

His alcohol-clouded, sleep-deprived mind kept trying to block out what happened, but every time he closed his eyes, he saw her. Vanessa, the love of his life, dead. The days after it happened were physically and emotionally draining. He was rushed to the hospital that night in shock. The next day, he was intermittently woken up to questions by the police, consolations from their friends, and the hardest visits of all when her family came in to talk to him.

What made it even worse was that they didn't blame him at all. But he wanted them to. He felt like it was all his fault. He constantly replayed that night in his head and wished more than anything that he could go back and change it. He could've told her not to go swimming or watched her when she did or jumped in with her. Admittedly, that last option would have resigned them to the same fate, but at least they would still be together.

He knew if his friends weren't constantly around, he might've tried to end the pain permanently instead of just masking it with large amounts of alcohol. He missed her so much.

In the days since being released from the hospital, just being awake was a struggle. He had taken to drinking from the moment he woke up until he inevitably blacked out at some point later in the day.

Part of him hoped that if he drank enough, he would see her again...but not the pale, dead version his mind kept showing him... the one that was so full of life it felt like everywhere she went, happiness followed. Just like her lifeless body, it felt like all color had drained from his life. Everything was in grayscale.

David knew that today was the day he needed to pull it together, even just for a few hours. This was going to be his last chance to say goodbye to the woman he loved.

He could go back to slowly killing himself tonight.

He peeled himself off the couch and started brewing a cup of coffee. The sweet, bitter smell sparked a memory that immediately went from pleasant to painful. He remembered how Vanessa would get up early for a yoga class every Sunday morning and turn on the coffee maker so that David would wake up to a hot cup of coffee.

He tried to fight back the tears, but they wouldn't stop. There was no aspect of his life that she didn't touch...His apartment that she was slowly moving into...His job that she used to come by during lunch so they could eat together...His friends that became her extended family...The beach...

How was he supposed to go on without the person who was such a large part of everything?

He tried burning the pain away with a scalding shower. It worked for a few minutes.

When he got out and dried off, he realized he was changing his clothes for the first time since getting home from the hospital. He grabbed the dirty clothes and brought them straight to the trash can in the kitchen.

David grabbed a mug and poured himself some freshly brewed coffee. His head was pounding from being completely emotionally drained and very, very hungover. He heard someone coming in and was surprised to see Melissa.

"What are you doing here?" He asked.

"Well, nice to see you too, bum." She responded.

"I'm sorry, Mel. Drew left a note that Jimmy was coming by, and I thought you were still out of town with JD." David's guilt was an ever-growing mass, taking over more and more of his body. It now spread to how he just talked to his friend.

"I was just messing with you, D. Sorry, you know I kinda suck with emotional stuff. I told JD I had to get back here, but he could enjoy the rest of the trip by himself if he wanted. He'll probably just end up golfing until coming home next week." She explained.

"You didn't have to cut your vacation short." More guilt. "I feel bad that you had to come here...for this." He had to sit down. He hated crying in front of other people. Always had. But try as he might, the last few days had him shedding tears at an inhuman rate, more when he was really drunk.

"D, there is no way I was going to not be there for my best friend. I couldn't even imagine the way you are feeling, but I know that you would drop everything to be there for me if the situation was reversed," she told him. And she was right.

David couldn't do anything but nod his head. She continued.

"Vanessa meant a lot to me too. And to Jimmy and Drew." She said.

"I know, Mel…" he said through his sobs. "She was amazing. I loved her so much. It just doesn't feel fair, you know?"

"It's not fair. I wish there were anything I could say to help but I know there's not." Mel's tears started now too.

"I just keep replaying that night in my head. She was right there, and then she was gone. I could've saved her if I just went in the water with her…" David couldn't contain it anymore. With his head in his hands, he cried. Hard.

"D, if you went in the water, then you would've drowned too. You know what the police said. The rip current that night was so strong that even if you tried to swim out and help her, neither of you would've made it, and there wouldn't have been anybody to call for help," he knew she meant well, but her words still stung.

"I would've rather died with her than had to go on alone," David said.

"You're not alone. And you never will be. Do you understand me? Look at me and tell me you got that, okay?" She pleaded.

He acquiesced, looked up through his bloodshot eyes, and nodded.

"No, I need you to tell me you know you're not alone. This is important, David," she was relentless.

David looked at her, "I understand. I'm not alone. I'm just going to need some time."

"I know you will, but you have people who love you immensely. We will be here every step of the way," she explained.

"Thank you, Mel. It means a lot to me. Seriously," he told her.

"You don't have to thank me, okay? Look, Jimmy's going to be here soon. Why don't we go grab a late breakfast when he gets here? Get you out of the house for a few. Just something low-key." She said.

"Probably a good idea. I may have drank a little this morning and could use some food to soak up some of the alcohol," he said.

"Good call. I'll drive. Are you ready to go? I'll call Jimmy and let him know we want to leave as soon as he gets here," she said.

"I will be. Just give me a couple minutes," he told her.

David went to the bathroom and splashed some water on his face. The tears had stopped, but he had a nagging feeling they would return without much notice.

When he returned to the living room, Jimmy was just coming in through the front door. Melissa had already put on her shoes, so David did the same.

"Hey man, look at you all cleaned up." Said Jimmy.

"Yeah, yeah, I know I kinda needed it. You guys should tell me next time I start putting off a stench like that." David said. His little chuckle almost brought on more tears.

"I was going to start by spraying you with some disinfectant, but I guess telling you would work, too. It's not as funny, though." Jimmy responded.

"If you guys are done being hilarious, can we go eat? I'm starving." Melissa said sarcastically.

The three friends went out to her car. David voluntarily sat in the back. He hadn't left the house much the last few days and was already worried about being able to control his tears.

The ride to the cafe was not easy. His head was constantly flooded with reminders of Vanessa: music on the radio, passing a liquor store where they used to go to pick up wine or beer before hanging out with his friends, and a billboard advertising one of her favorite stores.

It was all too much, and David broke down in the back seat.

"Hey, you okay, man? Should we head back home?" Jimmy asked.

Melissa added, "Maybe this is too much right now. We should just order something to go, and one of us can pick it up. "

"No, no, it's okay," David said through sobs. Again. "I can't hide inside the rest of my life, right? There's just so much that reminds me of her everywhere. I'm going to have to deal with it."

"Are you sure? We can go home and try this again another day," Mel asked.

"Let's just go. I'm pretty damn hungry, and I know you guys are too." David said. But he wasn't hungry, not in the least. His mind was being flooded with memories of Vanessa and he hoped that if he could just get used to them, maybe he could make it through the day.

They pulled up at the cafe. Thankfully, it was a bit off the beaten path, and David had never been there before. Melissa offered him some tissues. He wiped away his tears, and, even though his eyes were bloodshot and baggy, he felt like he could hold it together long enough to have a nice breakfast with his friends.

Wishful thinking.

Being out in public for the first time since losing Vanessa had many unforeseen challenges. It wasn't just all the things that kept reminding him of her. Those were already keeping his emotions on thin ice. But there were so many times that she would just pop into his head, and he would be reminded that she was gone. Little individual tortures. Seeing eggs Benedict on the menu and thinking —just for the briefest of moments—he will have to tell her about it and maybe they could come by here one morning to try it.

He tried to maintain composure but it was no use. The tears started up again.

"Guys, I'm really sorry, but I'm going to wait outside. I just need some air." He told his friends.

Once he was outside, his tears joined the warm, humid air. He sat down on the curb and let himself cry. He wasn't sure how he was supposed to go on like this. She was everywhere and nowhere, and it all hurt so much. He wanted to escape the pain, tell her he was sorry, and shut his mind off because he couldn't handle this.

He saw a liquor store across the street. He stood up, but as soon as he started taking a step forward, he heard Jimmy.

"Hey man, wait up. I'll come with you." He said.

"You don't need to do that. You should go eat your food. I just..." David trailed off, suddenly disappointed in himself.

"You just wanted to grab a drink because you're hurting, and the alcohol helps numb the pain. I totally get it, man." Jimmy told him.

"You don't know what this feels like. It's like I'm getting stabbed every time a thought of her comes into my mind, and the only time that knife is dulled is when I'm hammered. It's more than just the pain, though...it's like my life isn't complete anymore. Like its whole purpose is gone, and I'm just moving on autopilot." David told him through his unrelenting tears.

"There is no special trick to stop the pain or even help you get through the day. Dude, I know you will have a lot of bad days; there's no getting around that. Everything just takes time. But we are here to help you in any way that we can. We lost someone we cared about, too, and it sucks, but we all know what you lost. So, whatever you need, let us know and we will help. You want to drink yourself stupid? I'll drink with you. But can we wait until later?" Jimmy asked.

David sat back down on the curb, and Jimmy took a seat next to him. "Yeah, we can wait until later. I think I'm just not ready to be out in public yet. I see reminders of her everywhere."

"Probably a good call. I don't think you can escape them. You guys weren't exactly homebodies." Jimmy said.

He was right, though. David and Vanessa both loved being around other people and spent most nights either with friends or out exploring the city. There were very few cafes, dive bars, coffee shops, or eclectic restaurants that they didn't become regulars at. Finding a way to make it around here without having to see her everywhere he went was going to be a challenge and not one that David was up to conquer just yet.

David waited outside while Jimmy went and got Melissa and their food. He suddenly had a thought. He couldn't go anywhere around here without seeing her...but what if he went somewhere different? Somewhere they had never been before. Somewhere far away...

He shook off the thought. He had lived his whole life around here. Surely he could think of a less drastic solution.

The three friends started back to Drew's house. David picked at his food during the ride, trying his best to keep himself distracted from the ghosts of his life with Vanessa. It seemed an almost Sisyphean task. He was glad that Jimmy turned off the radio when the car started. No need to risk hearing some song that brought back a formerly happy memory. But it seemed any time he would glance out the car window, she was there. On a street they had walked before. In a store they had shopped in. At a park where they had kissed.

He held in the tears until it felt as if his eyes would burst.

Getting back to Drew's house finally offered him escape. He went to the bathroom and let the tears flow. Looking in the mirror, he begged for an end to the hurting. *Please, just make it stop. I miss you so fucking much, Vanessa. I don't feel like I can go on like this*, he said to himself.

He came out looking defeated. His concerned friends wanted to help, but all he wanted was to shut his mind down.

"Hey, I'm going to lay down for a bit. I just need to sleep off the last of this killer hangover". He told them.

"Okay. I'll wake you up in a couple of hours when we have to start getting ready." Jimmy told him.

David didn't want to think about what the afternoon would bring. He would have to say goodbye to her for the last time. Even that passing thought felt like his heart was being stabbed.

He went and laid down for a dreamless sleep.

Jimmy gently woke him up. "Hey man, we have to leave in a little bit, but I didn't want to wake you up too early."

David groggily responded. "Thanks, man. What time is it?"

"Like quarter till two. Mel's brewing some fresh coffee, and Drew is on his way." Jimmy told him.

"Alright, I'm getting up. I could use a cup." David replied.

David stretched out on the bed, looking up at the ceiling. The warm midday sun made the curtains glow, and he could feel the room warming up. The walls felt like they were slowly moving toward him. The ceiling too. He was suddenly feeling claustrophobic. He sat up and felt like his chest was tightening uncomfortably, and he wasn't sure if he was breathing right. Everything felt wrong. He was able to make it to the living room before dropping down on one knee and, barely speaking above a raspy whisper, asking for help.

Jimmy rushed over first. "Dude, what do you need? You need an ambulance?"

He put his arm around David's shoulder, helped him stand, and walked him to the couch. Melissa then came over with a cold washcloth and put it on his forehead.

"Hold that there for a few minutes." She told him.

David had heard people described as being a wreck before. Typically someone who had a string of bad luck or a rough weekend or had just gone through a bad breakup. But the thought had just entered his mind that none of those things held a candle to his current state. He wasn't just a wreck. He was the site of a huge explosion. A bomb had gone off in his life, and now was just the broken pieces of debris and shrapnel.

After a few minutes, he started feeling like he maybe wasn't about to die. Drew was walking him through some deep breaths and Jimmy grabbed him some cold water. "I'm going to be ok, guys. Thank you. Seriously."

"You sure, dude? Man, you were pale when you came out of the room." Drew said.

"He's getting his color back." Mel turned to David, "But, David, I think you should try and eat something before we go, okay?"

Go. Soon he would be going to see the woman he loved lowered into the ground. Every time that thought started growing in his mind, he still didn't believe it was real. It was like she was just away and would be back soon, and he couldn't accept any other explanation. But her last words kept coming back as a haunting reminder that she was gone, and he would have to find a way to make it without her:

Your loss.

"Still with us, D?" Mel asked. David was zoning out as thoughts of Vanessa kept clouding his mind.

"Yeah, I'm here. I'll eat something, and then I'll get ready to go, " he said emotionlessly. After the morning's events, he wasn't sure he had any tears left to cry.

"I'll make you an awesome grilled cheese; you just focus on getting ready," Drew told him.

His friends were patient with him, but he could tell they wanted to get going. They loved her too, and even though they were in pain, their focus was still on David. He hated himself more with every passing nice thing they did for him that he didn't feel he deserved. He kept coming back to the same fact.

Vanessa was gone because of him.

He did his best to quickly get ready to go, trying not to focus on what he was about to do. On especially bad days, he used to employ a mental trick: He would picture something much worse and then start to feel better, that at least his life wasn't that bad.

The problem now was he couldn't think of anything worse.

He finished up and grabbed the surprisingly tasty grilled cheese that Drew made for him. In a complete fog, he followed his friends to Drew's car. His mind couldn't handle what was happening and it shut down. It was like a computer running in safe mode. Essential functions worked, but there wasn't much going on with the processor. A big part of this was because of the route they had to take to the cemetery. Passing by places they frequented was bad enough this morning, but now they were going past places that were major parts of their relationship. The bar where they met. The restaurant where they had their first real date. An apartment they recently looked at together. If his brain were running at full speed, he would have broken down multiple times just on the car ride.

Fortunately, the fog didn't start lifting until they were already parked. Nobody rushed to get out of the car. The weight of the moment hung heavy in the air. The silence was broken first by Jimmy. He turned to David

"Hey man, just wanted to let you know that if it gets to be too much for you in there and you need to step out for some air, we're coming with you," Jimmy told him. Melissa and Drew nodded to show they agreed with that plan.

"Thanks, guys. But I'm going to make it. I owe it to her and her family," David said solemnly. But I am going to need some heavy hands pouring my drinks when we get home."

For the first time since that fateful night when Vanessa drowned, the four of them shared a laugh. It was brief and quickly forgotten under the burden of saying goodbye to an amazing person.

They made the difficult walk to the large crowd already forming around her casket. The closer they got, the more David's tears streamed down his cheeks. Jimmy put his arm around him.

When they reached the plot, Vanessa's family motioned for the friends to come stand with them near her soon-to-be grave. Her mom and dad hugged David, and he broke down even further. He wanted them to hate him as much as he hated himself for what he had let happen, but they didn't.

Her mother whispered to him, "We love you, and we know she did, too—more than anything."

He tried to speak, to tell her that he loved Vanessa beyond what words could properly convey, to say he was so sorry that he didn't save her. But he could barely breathe through his sobs and couldn't do anything but nod and bury his head in her shoulder.

As the service began and the pastor spoke, David couldn't hear a word of it. He couldn't stop thinking about the casket and how the woman he loved, the woman who was going to be his wife, who he was going to start a family with, was in there and would soon be lowered into the ground. He couldn't wrap his head around the fact that just a couple weeks ago, she was alive, and they were out doing things together and holding hands and kissing and talking, and now, now she was nothing more than a corpse in a box, and he would never have another memory with her again.

He didn't realize when the service was winding down until he snapped back to reality and noticed people were walking by the casket, saying their final goodbyes. He didn't want to. It felt too permanent. Once he said goodbye, then he had to accept that she was gone for good.

So he waited.

He watched as everyone else slowly made their way past her, most of them crying until all that remained were her closest family and the four friends.

David looked at them and said, "I think I'm going to stay here for a bit if you guys don't mind."

"No, stay as long as you need. You are more than welcome to come by our house for dinner. All of you can, if you want, " her dad said.

"You sure you don't want us to stay with you?" Melissa asked David.

"No, it's okay. I just need to talk to her one last time." He explained.

Drew told him, "Call us whenever you need a ride, and we'll come back to get you. "

And with that, the family and friends said their goodbyes to each other and left. David walked closer to Vanessa's casket. There were so many things he wanted to say but didn't know where to start. So, he stood there in silence. The wind was picking up, and some clouds had started rolling in.

Finally, he started:

"Vanessa, I'm so, so sorry. I should have tried to stop you from swimming that night. Or I should have gone with you. Either way, we would still be together right now. Instead, I have to say goodbye to you, and it's not fair. From the moment we met, I couldn't picture a life without you in it. I figured we would grow old together and have decades of great memories. Now, I'm stuck with these amazing few years worth of memories, but they only hurt whenever I think about them. I can't even leave the house because you are everywhere. I've got to figure out how to keep living, but I don't know how and I wish I could ask you because you always seemed to have a way to fix things. And dammit, I miss everything about you so much. I don't want to say goodbye. It should have been me who died that night. I know you loved me so much, but you were so much stronger than I was. You would find a way to spin it into something motivational. I can't do that, though. I don't even know if I can keep living here..." He trailed off as light raindrops began falling. The sky was transitioning from light gray clouds to some dark thunderheads. David could tell storms were coming but didn't care. He needed to say goodbye.

"I guess all I can say is that I love you. That I will always love you. But I think I need to leave this place to get away from all those beautiful memories I have of you. If I don't, I will end up joining you a lot sooner than I'm supposed to..." he suddenly felt calm. He was voicing something that had only been a brief thought before now. The only way he would survive without her was if he could get away from the ghost of their life together. And he could not do that in this town.

"I miss you more than words can say, Nessa. I would give anything to go back to that night and save you. But I need to say goodbye now." With those words, the sky opened up. Thunder clapped in the distance. David wept like he had never wept before.

In the pouring rain, David began walking out of the cemetery. He knew it was at least 10 miles to get back to Drew's place, but he welcomed the hours alone to say a silent goodbye to each of the memories he had with Vanessa on that long, dreary walk. He thought about the first night they met and how she kissed him at the bar. He remembered their first date the next week and how he was pretty sure he fell in love with her over dinner. One by one, he remembered as many of the times he had shared with Vanessa as he could. And after each one, he said goodbye to it, hoping to bury that memory in a faraway, dark recess of his mind.

It took four hours, but he found himself slowly walking up Drew's driveway, soaking wet from the heavy rain and constant tears. He still hadn't decided whether to tell his friends he was leaving, but he knew he needed to leave soon. There was no other way. He had enough money in the bank to last a few months.

He realized he could leave tomorrow, just pack up the necessities, and drive north. He didn't even feel like this was a choice; he had to do it if he wanted to stay alive.

He walked into the house and was nearly knocked over by his friends.

"Dude, where the hell were you? Why haven't you answered your phone?" Jimmy asked with an impatient, but genuinely concerned tone.

"Seriously! We were getting so worried. I drove to the cemetery twice looking for you. We were just about to call the police. " Melissa told him.

"I'm sorry, guys. I turned my phone off when it started pouring and wanted to walk back here. I had a lot to think about." David explained.

"We totally get that, D. Just keep us in the loop next time, okay? We weren't sure if something happened to you, " Melissa continued.

"I will. But for now, can I please have a towel and a bottle of something strong?" He asked.

The four friends spent the next few hours drinking and talking and, for the first time since Vanessa's death, some actual laughing.

Not a ton. It was still a mostly somber occasion. But there were moments when guards were let down, and happiness broke through.

None of that changed David's already made-up mind. He would be leaving in the morning.

After hours of drinking heavily, the friends began slowly calling it a night. David stumbled his way to the guest room and fell back on the bed. He was unconscious as soon as his head hit the pillow.

32

David opened his eyes back on the couch. This time, when he returned from the story, he was alone. He lay there, trying to get a grip on everything he just learned. Reliving the day that Vanessa was buried was almost as bad as the day she drowned. He had to feel all that pain again, fresh. Both types of pain. The sudden, soul-crushing hurt of seeing the person you love die and the drawn-out, tear-ridden hurt of saying goodbye. Both memories had been locked away for so long that it was like having a deep wound reopened with some salt thrown into it for good measure. The guilt. The sadness. The complete desperation. The feeling of losing someone you love and knowing that you could have saved them.

But now David understood why Matthew wanted him to live this day again. He got the message buried under all that pain.

His friends never left his side. They helped him get through one of the hardest days of his life, and even though they lost someone they cared about too, they focused so much on just helping David get through it. And how did David thank the people that loved him so much?

By abandoning them.

He wished he could go back to that night when he lost everything. He knew that if he could just get a do-over, so much of his life would have been better. He would save Vanessa and marry her, and Drew and Jim would be the best men, and they would all live the rest of their lives down by the beach. Melissa would live near them with her family. They would all take vacations together. Maybe there would be a bunch of kids who all got to grow up together as second-generation friends.

But he knew that life would never exist.

In its place was the life of David's choices. Loneliness. Sadness. Despair. Hopelessness. And then he realized something about all of it. He may have pushed all the painful memories to the darkest recesses of his mind, but he never escaped them. He had been living the life he felt he deserved. The guilt from Vanessa's death drove all his decisions away from the people he loved because he knew he couldn't go through losing anyone again.

He was living a selfish life filled with a quiet fear of an unspeakable pain.

There was a certain irony to finally realizing that your miserable life was completely built by your own terrible choices while you were on the edge of death in a deep coma. The only positive he could find in this dreadfully depressing situation was that he could go back into his library and relive all the happiest moments from his past. He looked out at the expansive collection of books and thought about how he could see Vanessa, and hold her, and talk to her anytime he wanted.

But none of it would bring her back. Their relationship would always have an expiration date, a point at which all their plans for the future would cease. Struggling between the happiness of reliving the days with her and the sadness of its tragic end, David decided he needed to talk to Matthew.

He got up and explored a little bit while looking for him. He slowly walked down the aisles, pairing the shades of the books with different parts of his life. The books were pretty much the same in the first couple of rows. This was when his days basically became carbon copies of each other. Nothing set them apart. Work. Home. Sleep. Repeat. If it wasn't for the car crash, Matthew could have just copied one over and over and gone on a nice vacation.

The next aisle finally trended toward being a shade or two lighter, but it was only a small, hardly noticeable change. However, there were a few even lighter books mixed in there. Those must have been the days he started going out on hikes and exploring or the days he would get a call from Drew, Jim, or Melissa.

As he walked on, he knew he was coming to the place where the books he had just visited were from. The shelves before the missing places were lighter than the others, but after, they were so dark that they appeared as velvety shadows. The entire rest of the aisle was like this—hundreds of books representing hundreds of terrible days.

He walked a few aisles further. College. So many good days. Some bad ones too, but they were few and far between. That fit with how he remembered them. Some shelves were darker, and he figured they must have been when he struggled to find jobs or had money issues. Still, none of the days seemed that bad because he always had his friends, and the shelves reflected that. Any particularly dark book was immediately followed by a lighter one, and he knew that was because his friends always seemed to know when he needed them, and they would be there with some crazy fun plans.

There weren't many darker trends until around book 5500. He was about 15. Those years were such a mix of happiness and sadness and frustration and anger and hope. He couldn't remember all the details anymore, but some events stuck in his mind. His first heartbreak. The first time he drove with no one else in the car. Losing his virginity. The massive blowout fight with his dad. Camping with his friends. The books reflected these ups and downs well, with sudden color changes from light to dark and back again.

Walking on, he reached his early years. Hardly any books that weren't at least shaded slightly lighter than average. The first darker shades popped up around book number 1900, and after some quick math, he remembered that was when he moved to a new town and had to make new friends. But the shelves were still predominantly lighter shades over the next couple of aisles. His childhood was pretty good.

He moved past these and returned to where it all started. As he turned past the last bookshelf, the desk came into view. He could see Matthew sitting there waiting for him.

With a very serious look, he looked right at David, motioned to the chair next to the desk, and said, "David, I think that we should talk."

I knew it was time and didn't want it to be. He had so many lessons to learn, but I couldn't fight the facts of what was happening anymore. It was, quite literally, now or never.

David had heard that sentence spoken on various occasions throughout his life but could not remember when the result was ever a happy conversation. But with everything happening here, he didn't see how things could get any worse. He nodded and took a seat in the chair.

33

David came over and sat down in the same chair where we first spoke. As much as I hoped we would have more time, that he would get to savor a few more good memories, I knew that time was not a luxury we had. David would have to make the biggest choice of the rest of his life, and it had to be his own, and it had to be now. All I could do was be there to support him.

Matthew tried to explain the situation as accurately as he could. "As with most things in life, there is some good and some bad. While you have been here, reliving some of the very best and very worst times of your life, your body has been slowly healing. You still have a long road to recover from your devastating accident fully, but much of the pain has diminished while your bones have begun to mend. That is the good news."

He continued more somberly, "Your mind, however, has not been healing the same way, and unfortunately, it will not survive much longer without you taking back control."

"What does that mean exactly?" David asked.

"It means that if you stay here much longer, you will never wake up back in the real world," Matthew responded.

"What if I don't want to go back? Am I just going to wake up, no matter what?" He asked. He didn't want to go back. Not yet.

Matthew had prepared for this line of questioning. "It is possible for you to wake up. But it is also just as possible that you have reached the end of your story. It may sound cliched, but ultimately that choice will be yours to make."

David looked confused. "I don't understand…how do I just decide if I want to live or die?"

"It is a bit more complicated than that," Matthew opened the desk drawer and pulled out his pencil. "This looks like a completely normal pencil. However, with this pencil, the entire story of your life has been written. Up until now, the way it has worked has been you live your life, and I write it all down. That won't work for this situation. You need to be the author of what comes next."

David needed a little more clarification. "What do you mean?"

"The time has come for you to make a choice, David. Do you stay here, reliving all of your happiest days for as long as you wish before moving on to what comes next? Or, do you want to wake up and begin the arduous process of recovery but with having a chance to change the rest of your story?" Matthew asked him.

David wasn't ready for this. That life he was living was painful, with distant friends and his days spent doing the same thing over and over. And now, he would have to do all that with the physical pain of the accident and the emotional pain of suddenly having the memories of Vanessa back.

But that life was real. It wasn't written. And the choices he would make every day mattered. There was weight tied to every decision.

He wanted to walk back through the books and relive just a few more good days before deciding. "Can I stay here just a little longer?" David asked.

Matthew somberly shook his head. "I'm afraid that staying here any longer will remove the choice of waking back up. You see, your mind has been teetering on the edge of a cliff, so to speak. We have reached a point where you must decide if you will let it go for good."

"What happens to you if I decide to go back?" David asked.

"I will still be here, chronicling the rest of your days, being that voice in your head telling you to be a good person and find happiness. Hoping beyond all hope that you start letting people back into your life and allowing me to add more to the good days you'll want to relive when you do finally pass on from your time on Earth," he said.

David was weighing his options. He had learned enough here to not take this choice lightly. "And if I do decide to stay here?"

"I will still be here until the day your Earthly body dies. At that point, I'll be your guide to what comes next," Matthew explained.

"And I have to decide right now?" David asked.

Matthew answered. "I'm afraid so."

Damn, why can't anything just be easy, David thought. There were so many books of his happiest days here that he could spend an eternity just going back and choosing from them. He could also see Vanessa again. But what would she say, knowing he tortured himself for so long and then just gave up?

He knew that if he went back, his life would be hard. But, there was a chance, small as it might be, that he could create new "best days". He was torn, being pulled apart by the gravity that each decision carried. His life had been a struggle for so many years, and if he had been told when he first got here that he had to choose between staying and going back, he would have stayed and relived all his favorite days over and over and never even given it a second thought. But now he knew that his friends were out there and they missed him and that it was his choices that kept making things so rough for him. What if he could turn things around?

The question that kept coming back to him, though, was what Vanessa would ask him to do. The girl who loved everybody and made him so happy for so long...deep down, he knew exactly what she would say.

"You know, when I look back now, I think the best way to explain it is that the person I wanted to be, the person I knew I could be, was on the top of a mountain, and every day I tried to get a little closer to being him. Sometimes I'd stumble and fall a little bit, but when I had my friends around, they would catch me, and I'd get right back on the climb. Then when I moved away, there was no one to stop the fall, and I've been down at the bottom for so long that I forgot all about that person on the top of the mountain," David explained. He remembered Vanessa's words at the bar.

He realized there was still so much he wanted to do. He wasn't ready for his story to be over.

"I think what I'm trying to say is I want to go back," he told Matthew.

Matthew smiled broadly. David noticed what seemed to be a tear slide down his cheek. "I'm very happy that you have made that choice, David."

"But I don't want to forget all this. I learned so much here. Will I remember it? Will I remember you?" He knew that he couldn't go back and just add physical pain to what his life was like before.

"Yes, David, you will. Not all of it, mind you. Others would write off the memories you do retain as just being the crazy dreams of someone with a severe head injury. Not that they would be very far off from the truth," Matthew winked.

David smiled at that thought. "Ok, well, how do I wake up?"

"You'll need to take this pencil and this blank book…" Matthew put them down in front of him. "…and just start writing about waking up."

David sat there for a moment thinking. He knew no words could properly express his gratitude, but he wanted to try. "Look, I need to thank you. When the accident happened, my life was completely lonely, and I was okay with that because of how long it had been since I had anyone in it. You showed me that I was never truly alone and that even out there, there are still people who care about me. I want to make sure you know how much you've helped me."

My eyes gave away how much that meant to me. I was going to miss being able to talk to David like this, but he had a chance to make choices to better his life, and I was ecstatic to have played a role in that.

"I have always strived to guide you in a way that led to happiness and kindness. The choices of others hardened you, and that made happiness such a difficult daily proposition. But you have always had the ability to change your path. Knowing that you see that now brings me more joy than you will ever know."

David opened the book in his lap. He was staring at a blank page for the first time since arriving in his library. He thought for a moment before starting…

"And then I opened my eyes…"

34

And then David opened his eyes.

He lay there, wincing at the sudden onslaught of bright, fluorescent lighting. Once his eyes slowly adjusted, he realized he was staring up at a ceiling, his mind taking its time processing the situation. He could see his hospital room for the first time. He looked around, and the sterile whiteness of the room stung, but he didn't want to close his eyes again. Everything was transitioning from blobs of light and color to blurry shapes to a gradual sharpening of lines, allowing him to start making out his surroundings. He saw a row of, most likely, "Get Well Soon" cards on a table nearby, although it just as well could've been colorful boxes or books. Identifying the fresh flowers that lined the window sill was much easier. Their scent was beautiful. He took a deep breath and wondered if this was all real.

He could hear the familiar beeps coming from his heart monitor, which brought back a flood of memories of Matthew, the books, his friends, Vanessa, the good days, and the terrible ones. He remembered the library and how much Matthew cared about him.

He closed his eyes for just a moment and whispered a brief, simple message that he knew would be written in today's book.

"Thank you, Matthew."

It must have been either early morning or late afternoon because the sun's rays flooded through the window, casting long, flower-shaped shadows onto his bed. The room was currently empty. But he didn't feel alone. He knew it would be his choice if he ever truly felt alone again. A small smile crept onto his face.

He was quietly taking an account of all his current aches and pains. Thankfully, there didn't seem to be too many. That is until he tried to turn to see the door to his room. *Okay, mental note, don't do that again.* Everything felt stiff and brittle. He had heard the door open and footsteps coming up to the side of the bed. A nurse walked up to check on the devices connected to his arm. She hadn't looked over at him yet. He decided to try speaking.

"Good morning, I think," he spoke in a voice that felt like it was being said with a sandpaper tongue. Damn, he needed some water.

The strange noise coming from the previously comatose patient startled the nurse terribly, and she jumped back and looked like she might scream. *My bad*, David thought.

"Just a second…" She said as she went quickly to the door and called for a doctor.

David lay there, and the smile that had crept onto his face decided it didn't want to leave just yet.

It was only a minute or two before the nurse returned with a doctor who couldn't hide his surprise very well. There were so many questions and tests and even when David started feeling so very tired, he did not dare go back to sleep. Not yet, anyway. There would be plenty of time for that later. For now, he wanted to take everything in. It was such a strange feeling. It was like he was just starting his life all over but with a newfound treasure trove of memories and lessons already lived and learned. He held tight to the idea that he could make choices to shape it however he wanted.

More than anything, what he wanted right now was to see the people he cared about most. The people that cared about him even when he stopped caring about himself.

After what felt like an eternity, the nurse returned and said he was cleared to have some visitors. David expected that meant that when people learned he was awake, they would make the trip back up to see him. As luck would have it, the nurse said someone was already waiting to see him.

In came his mother. She was crying. She came right up to him and held his face like he was still just a little boy. David started crying too. No words were spoken, but they weren't needed.

David broke the silence first by simply saying, "I'm sorry, Mom."

She wiped away her tears, "Oh, there is nothing to be sorry for, David. It was an accident. I have prayed and prayed and prayed, and I am just so happy that you are awake now. That is all that matters."

David gave a quick laugh. It hurt a little, and he grimaced but smiled back as he responded, "Guess I just needed some sleep. Nothing to worry about."

"You know, that is not funny," she said. Well, there are some other people here to see you, too. Can I bring them in?"

David was suddenly very curious and hopeful. "Wait, who else is here?"

"A few friends who came a long way and refused to go home," she laughed."Jimmy, Drew, and Melissa. They have been coming back every weekend. They were actually about to head to the airport when the doctor called for me. When I told them you woke up, they canceled their flights and headed right over."

David couldn't help but start tearing up again. He didn't deserve friends like this. But he wasn't going to take them for granted ever again. He stiffly wiped away the tears from his face. His arm now ached, but he couldn't care less.

He looked at his mom. "How do I look?"

"Oh, you look fine, all things considered. I'm going to get them," she said.

His three best friends came in. It was strange. He felt like he just spent so much time with them, even though he hadn't seen them in years. They still looked the same too, except for a few gray hairs and the emergence of a couple of wrinkles around the eyes.

Jim's deep voice spoke first, "Ho-ly shit. Welcome back to the land of the living, Davy."

David laughed, "Still with the 'Davy'? And anyway, I was only almost dead!"

"You know, you had us pretty freaked out, man. I was starting to think you were just gone for good," Drew said. Melissa gave him a stern look.

"Well, I knew you would wake up at some point. There was no way you were going to die all alone up here," Melissa chimed in. She smiled, and David remembered kissing her at the beach. It felt like just a few days ago but in a completely separate lifetime.

"Yeah, as soon as we heard what happened, we knew we had to make a trip. Your mom called Mel and set everything up," Drew added

"Thanks, guys. It means a lot to me to wake up and see you here," David told them. His doctor returned and told his visitors they had to wrap things up. More tests were needed, and he advised David to take things easy for a few days.

"You heard the doctor. We better head out for now. But we will be extending this trip a bit. You just need to get your strength back, and then we can get you home," Mel told him.

"Can't wait. I better be seeing you guys soon," David told them.

"Definitely, man. We won't be far," Answered Jim.

The friends said their goodbyes and left. David's mom came over to his bed and gave him a painful but welcome hug before saying her goodbyes as well. The rest of the day was spent napping and answering questions from the doctors. At some point, he wasn't sure exactly when he fell into a deep sleep. He couldn't quite remember the dreams in the morning, but he woke up with a smile. It felt like he was getting reacquainted with an old friend. He didn't dwell on that thought much, though. It had been over a month since he had a normal night of sleeping followed by a normal wake up, so he figured that must have been the cause.

It took another couple of days before the hospital would release him. They wanted to err on the side of caution when it came to his brain injury. Besides a mild, nagging headache, he wasn't very bothered by it. Finally, when they felt comfortable with the test results, they allowed him to be checked out. His friends came together in their rental car, and after another round of big hugs from all 3 of them, they headed out to lunch. His mom was already there waiting for them.

"I just have to tell you guys, thank you. I've missed having you around more than you know." David tried fighting back the tears as much as he could, but it was useless.

He composed himself enough to continue. "After everything happened with Vanessa, I ran. But I shouldn't have. It's taken me this long even to be able to talk about it. If I had stayed down there, it would've been harder at first, but I know I wouldn't have repressed things the way I did. Mistakes were made."

His friends exchanged surprised looks. He hadn't so much as said her name in over a decade.

"You did what you felt like you had to, man. None of us could have imagined going through what you went through," Drew told him while Mel and Jim nodded their agreement.

"Honestly, I wasn't sure if you were ever going to get past it," Jim said.

"I don't think I'll ever get past it. I'm not sure that's possible. But I can't spend the rest of my life running from those memories. She was an awesome person, and I loved her so damn much, and she's just gone. It wasn't fair to her for me to live like none of that happened," David explained.

The friends spent the rest of the car ride talking about Vanessa's quirky traits, mostly smiling and laughing, although they shed tears on several occasions. Finally, they arrived at the restaurant, where David, his friends, and his mom spent hours catching up.

David, even through the roller coaster of emotions he had experienced during his coma, was feeling like his future was wide open. He couldn't go back to being the guy who closed himself to anything that might end up hurting. Embracing his newfound ability to choose happiness, he made himself a promise.

I will be living every day as best I can. No more excuses.

After lunch, his friends gave him a ride to his apartment. They were heading to the airport afterward but promised to come back in a couple of weeks to check-in.

He knew they would.

35

One year later.

EHHHH-EHHHH-EHHHHH-EHH...

David reached over and turned off his alarm. The room was dark, and the whirring of the fan overhead gave the impression that a gentle breeze was caressing him awake. He stretched his arms out wide and kicked the covers off. He could still remember parts of his dream. He was in a library. The same one he often dreamt about. He was talking to a nice old man. He couldn't remember all the details but knew it was pleasant.

He got out of bed and, with a still slightly noticeable limp, went to his window. The sun was only slightly above the horizon, but the rays of light that cut between the trees danced on the glistening, dew-covered grass. The morning mist held the rays in place, and they looked like long, ghostly hands reaching out from the sky. He opened the window and took a deep breath. The smell of the freshly blooming magnolias not far from his window rose to meet him.

He had moved into a spare room in Jimmy's house shortly after leaving the hospital, but not before taking his boss up on that offer to go out for a drink. Everyone from the office was there. Even though he wasn't quite at 100% yet, he had a great time. He promised his boss that they would stay in touch; this time, it wasn't just an empty gesture. They checked in with each other every couple weeks and Tom is coming down to visit with his family next month.

Returning to Florida allowed him to close the book on his life with Vanessa properly. Shortly after arriving, he visited her grave. He told her about the few foggy memories of his conscience and the hidden books he couldn't remember and said he was sorry for not knowing what to do about it. But he went on to say that the thought of her finally saved him, that he knew she wouldn't want him to stop living.

He was going to live his life to the fullest the way she would have wanted him to.

David slowly walked to the living room. The savory smell of freshly cooked bacon hit him and immediately made his mouth water. He wasn't used to Jimmy cooking. Hopefully, he made enough to share.

When he rounded the corner, he was pleasantly surprised to see Melissa.

"I hope you're hungry! Jimmy was working early today, so I asked if I could come by and make you breakfast. I hope you don't mind," she said.

"Bacon? Hell no, I don't mind," David said with a smile. "You need a hand?"

"Sure! How good are you with pancakes? I already made the batter, and the griddle is warming up," she told him.

"I think I can handle pouring batter onto a griddle," David laughed.

David and Melissa worked together to make a great breakfast, and then they sat and talked while they ate. Over the last couple of months, they had been spending more and more time together. However, they never really made plans. Everything was spontaneous, and David loved it.

"So you up for the beach today?" She asked him. It had taken him a few months before he could go back there. Not the one from that night. He was pretty sure he wouldn't ever be going back to that one. But he was happy to finally feel his toes in the sand and hear the crashing of the waves, followed by the gentle murmur of the water rushing up the sand. The salty air filled his lungs with a feeling he could never really explain.

He was always ready to go back now.

"Yeah, the weather's supposed to be great," he said.

"Awesome. I'll see if Drew and the family are around," she responded.

"Wait, how about just me and you go?" David felt like a nervous teenager all over again.

When she smiled, Melissa looked slightly blushed and said, "Oh, you mean like a date? Are you trying to ask me on a date, Davy?"

She loved putting him on the spot. David couldn't help but laugh along with her. "Yeah, you know, maybe I am. Is that alright?"

She smiled softly and said, "Fine by me. Just don't tell your mom. I don't need her blowing up my phone telling me I better treat her little boy right."

With that, they both laughed some more. After everything he had been through, David finally felt like he was alive again. He had his friends back (even though they never really left him), he was back home and made peace with his past.

It was going to be a great day.

Epilogue

The changes that David made and how his life played out after waking up made me realize how important our time together was and how confronting his past head-on allowed him to finally move past it. Even with little memory of our interactions, he was able to take the bits and pieces, along with the clearer recollections of his previous choices, and gain a level of happiness that he had previously turned away from. It took all the pain of reliving the loss of his fiancé to finally make peace with his choices.

Now, I have gone back to simply chronicling his time on Earth while being a quiet and hopefully helpful voice in the back of his head. I like to think that he gives a little more weight to my advice when he hears me now, even if he doesn't fully know why. I know that this wasn't an easy path, but a few of us are blessed with those. And he still wanders off of it now and then. But he knows the path is there and always finds his way back to it.

One day, hopefully not for many, many years, I look forward to him spending all the time he wants going back through all his best memories and most joyous days. I will be there, after facing whatever punishments await me, as an old friend to point out all the great memories he was able to add because of his choice to pursue them. Until then, I will keep adding to his library.

See you in the afterlife.

Misplaced and Forgotten

Misplaced and Forgotten

About the Author

W.J. Thompson grew up in the South, moving between Georgia and Florida, with his two brothers. Most of his childhood was spent outdoors, exploring the woods, swimming in canals, and having to be pulled, kicking and screaming, away from the beach. He relocated to Massachusetts after receiving his history degree from the University of Central Florida and has reluctantly stayed through the harsh winters and lack of palm trees.

Over the last twenty years, he has dreamed of being a writer. After dealing with a lifelong affliction of procrastination and self-doubt, he made himself a promise to finally finish a story.

He enjoys many hobbies ranging from getting lost while hiking, clumsily playing soccer, painting poorly, and, of course, daydreaming. Being an attentive father to his two sons is his proudest accomplishment.

www.ingramcontent.com/pod-product-compliance
Lightning Source LLC
LaVergne TN
LVHW031611060526
838201LV00065B/4810